The Glassblower's Children

by Maria Gripe

WITH DRAWINGS BY
Harald Gripe

translated from the Swedish by
Sheila La Farge

The New York Review Children's Collection
New York

THIS IS A NEW YORK REVIEW BOOK
PUBLISHED BY THE NEW YORK REVIEW OF BOOKS
435 Hudson Street, New York, NY 10014
www.nyrb.com

Originally published in Swedish as *Glasbåsarns barn*
by Albert Bonners Förlag, Stockholm

Library of Congress Cataloging-in-Publication Data
Gripe, Maria, 1923–2007.
[Glasblåsarns barn. English]
The glassblower's children / by Maria Gripe ; illustrated by Harald
Gripe.
pages cm. — (New York Review children's collection)
Originally published in Stockholm, Sweden by Albert Bonniers Forlag
in 1964; English translation published in New York by Delacorte Press/
Seymour Lawrence in 1973.
Summary: The glassblower and his wife live happily until the prophecy
that their children will disappear comes true.
ISBN 978-1-59017-728-0 (hardback)
[1. Fairy tales.] I. Gripe, Harald, 1921- illustrator. II. Title.
PZ8.G886Gl 2014
[Fic]—dc23
2013044619

ISBN 978-1-59017-728-0
Also available as an electronic book: ISBN 978-1-59017-745-7

Cover design by Louise Fili Ltd.

Printed in the United States on acid-free paper.
1 3 5 7 9 10 8 6 4 2

Part
One

*"He who does not
foresee his fate
can live lightheartedly."*

HAVAMAL

I

THEY LIVED IN a poor old village called Nöda, which doesn't exist any more, in the misty county of Diseberga. Albert the glassblower had been born nearby, but his wife came from the north. Her name was Sofia and she was truly as beautiful to look upon as a rose.

Their children were given the names Klas and Klara. It was Albert who named them to remind him of his work, because Klas rhymed with glass and Klara turned his thoughts to clarity.

Albert was very poor, but he owned the cottage they lived in and the glassmaking workshop, too. It was a terribly small cottage. All the space along one wall inside was taken up by a sofa and an old clock. On the other side of the room stood a chest of drawers and a cupboard and between them a table in front of the window. Albert and Sofia slept on the sofa and the children in the chest of drawers.

The open fireplace was very wide and took up a

lot of room. Here by the hearth Sofia kept her spinning wheel. Over it a cradle hung from two iron hooks in the ceiling. The children had rocked in that cradle when they were tiny, but now it was where Sofia hid things she wanted to keep for herself.

Right next to the fireplace a door opened into a room containing a clothes chest and a stool. That was all.

Nor was the workshop much bigger, but both Albert and his assistant had enough space to work in, and Klas and Klara too, when they came to watch, and that was all that mattered.

Now, the glassware blown here was the finest you would ever see. Albert was a great artist with glass. However, when it came to selling any, he wasn't very successful. He traveled to the market place both in the autumn and the spring, but he never sold much. So it turned out that they were always struggling to make ends meet and never had a crumb left over.

When autumn came around, Sofia would go to the neighboring farmers and beat their harvested flax. She would take the children with her, and all three of them would be fed during the day. Sofia received a sheaf of flax and a round loaf of bread in payment for a day's work, and then they would live extravagantly.

Klas was the younger child, only a year old. He couldn't walk yet, but he would sit for hours watching his father blow glass. As easily as a child will blow soap bubbles, Albert shaped shimmering goblets and glittering bowls. But they didn't break like soap bubbles, they lasted: They were displayed in long rows on the shelves, and how they shone! It was like a miracle.

Klas sat still as a mouse in his corner and watched one glistening bubble after another swell up, conjured out of Albert's long glassblowing pipe. Klas thought about them as they were swung over his head, taking shape, growing large. A gaze full of

longing brightened his eyes as if he'd seen something far, far away. What could he see? What was he thinking about? Was it the heavens or the ocean, perhaps? He didn't know, he was too little to find the right words. But Albert smiled. He knew, it was the same with him. It was the beauty they saw.

Klara was some years older. She also liked to be in the workshop, but she never wanted to sit still. So this or that piece of glass fell to the floor when she was there, and crashed into a thousand pieces. It didn't bother her very much, she'd dance right out of the hut and run off home. At home hung the blond lengths of flax that Klara thought were most wonderful.

But Klas was beside himself every time a piece of glass broke. First he was delighted by the jingling crash, then he looked terrified and started crying when he saw the fragments on the floor. He was heart-broken and had to be carried away from there. Sometimes Albert even lost his temper because he thought Klas really should be getting used to the idea that glass does, sometimes, break. But Klas didn't. Quite the contrary. He sobbed and sobbed more each time, and finally Albert hardly dared let him visit the workshop.

So this was Klas' odd weakness, but no one paid too much attention to it because there were other things to think about.

Albert thought about glass. Only about glass. Glass in all shapes. Glass of all descriptions. Glitter-

ing, lustrous, mirroring, tinkling, ringing, crystal-
pure . . . glass. Always GLASS.

In fact, Sofia thought that Albert thought too
much about glass. She thought he liked glass more
than he liked her. The sun could rise and set, and the
moon too, with Albert still in his workshop blowing
glass. She would sit by the window staring out, waiting. Yes, that often happened. . . .

But Klara was always happy. How could she not
be, for she was Klara, who had a length of flax to
braid and a piece of a broken mirror to see herself in.
This was more than enough for her.

And so Klas' odd little weakness was kept to himself. No one understood the simple truth: Klas had realized that what is most beautiful must also be most fragile. Now this is scary and hard to bear when you are little and don't know anything about the nature of glass. For it is very upsetting that the most beautiful things in life shatter so easily.

But no one else was brooding over it. Least of all Sofia, who began to think dangerous thoughts. Discouragement and displeasure grew within her. One night when Albert came home from the workshop he found her crying by the window. She was sitting in the dark—she hadn't even lit a candle. The moonlight shone dimly upon her, and her tears glistened on the windowsill. She didn't look up.

"What in heavens! You're sitting here crying!" Albert said, distressed.

She sniffled her answer, "I feel so lonely when you're never home."

Then Albert explained that he was making a very special bowl. She just had to be patient a little longer and then he would be able to stay at home more often.

But Sofia sighed. She knew very well how it would be, she said. When the wonderful bowl was finished, Albert would think up something even more wonderful. She knew him by now. He would never make a bowl beautiful enough; he would never have time for her. . . .

8

Albert didn't know what to tell her. He stood there, completely at a loss, and realized there was some truth in what Sofia said.

"But you've got the children," he finally replied. "After all, you're not really alone." But he shouldn't have said that. And then Sofia shouldn't have let herself answer as she did.

"The children!" she spat out angrily. "What kind of company do you think they are? They're more trouble than anything else. . . ."

She didn't really mean what she said—no mother could—she regretted her words immediately. She was so proud and happy about her children. She only said it because, for just that moment, the dangerous thoughts had taken over. Albert looked grim, despairing, and neither of them said any more.

But Sofia reproached herself bitterly. She never forgot what she had said, and she was convinced that everything that happened afterwards was a punishment for those frightful words that had slipped out of her.

2

A LITTLE WAY outside the village there rose a pretty green hill. You could see it whichever way you walked; the village seemed to be resting comfortably in its protection.

An ancient apple tree grew on the hill. It drew everyone's attention; spring, summer, fall, and winter, it patterned itself against the sky, turned green, blossomed, burdened its branches with fruit, or sketched them bare, cold black. Everyone gazed up at it and thought how peaceful it looked.

And yet people said that it was a weird and terrible place. At one time it had been a Gallows Hill. Criminals had been brought there to be punished. And people said that as many criminals had met their fates on that hill as the tree bore fruit. Every autumn it was heavy with shiny red apples, but no one had ever succeeded in counting them.

The apples were delicious, and it was very, very long ago that the place had been a Gallows Hill.

Part One

Now someone lived there, though no one could understand why she wanted to or how she dared. You could just catch a glimpse of the little cottage. The apple tree hid it, but at night you could see a light up there.

This person was old, and wonderfully odd. Her name was Flutter Mildweather, or so she was called, for no one knew what she had been christened.

She got the name Flutter from the fact that she always walked about wearing a big indigo cloak with a shoulder cape. The deep, scalloped edge flapped like huge wings on her shoulders. And on her head she wore a very remarkable hat. Its flower-strewn brim belled out beneath a high violet peak decorated with butterflies.

She got the name Mildweather simply because people thought she promised and brought mild winds and gentle thaw. And, indeed, she rarely walked outside in winter time: Weeks could go by without her being seen. But then, suddenly, she would appear, fluttering down the hillside in her odd cape and flower-strewn hat, and then everyone knew they could expect mild weather. For though it might be thirty degrees below freezing, and the snow packed deep and firm, when Flutter Mildweather came, days of thaw were bound to follow. She was the surest sign of spring in the whole district.

Yes, Flutter was extraordinary in many ways. She could also tell fortunes. She scorned cards, but willingly predicted the future from people's hands and in the dregs of their coffee cups. And many people braved the terrors of Gallows Hill to creep up after dark and ask about their fates.

But fortune-telling wasn't Flutter Mildweather's task in life. Her real work was weaving. She wove carpets. The patterns of these she invented herself, and each had its own special theme. She sat at her loom day in and day out, brooding somewhat anxiously about the people and the life down in the village. And then one day she discovered that she knew what was going to happen to them. She could see it in the carpet design that grew under her hands. There she sat, looking into the future. It was like reading in a book, so plainly and clearly could she follow the events.

Now she thought all this was just as it should be, for such things didn't astonish Flutter Mildweather. Why, if she could sit down and predict the future by tracing the lines in a person's hand or staring into coffee dregs, should she be surprised to see patterns of the future in her carpets? So it came about that suddenly she would know how to go on weaving the pattern on which she was working. And in this way each task contributed to the other. The weaving and the fortune-telling blended together and, in a mysterious way, became two sides of the same thing.

But she would never tell from what secret source she received her knowledge about a person's fate or a carpet's design. Perhaps she didn't know herself. Whatever the truth might be, everyone in the village got on well with Flutter Mildweather.

Now it must be said that she neither wove nor told fortunes just to make money. She supported herself, and anything beyond that didn't interest her.

Though she sat at her loom constantly, she never had more than a few completely finished carpets on hand. But these were always very beautiful and special. And at the country fairs she always sat in her little tent and told fortunes, with the carpets hanging out on view.

And much could be said about Flutter Mildweather's eyes, for they were changing all the time and had great power over people. The most incredible, improbable quality of her eyes was gentleness, for they were like flowers; but their gentleness made it clear that they were not dangerous to look upon. Actually, she fixed the world and its people with a stare that was blue as wild mint flowers, those fragile little blossoms one finds in the grass in June. That was what Flutter Mildweather's eyes were like.

Yes, she was a most unusual person. . . .

People often have cats in the country as house pets. Or dogs. Flutter Mildweather had a raven. Wise Wit was his name. It is not known how she got

hold of him—whether she caught him herself, for instance—but she'd always had him, and he was a very remarkable creature.

He could talk. And he didn't chatter just any old nonsense, either. He answered directly and very wisely—that is, if he felt like it. Sometimes he didn't want to talk, for he could be quite temperamental. And sometimes he talked in riddles so that ordinary people couldn't make any sense out of it—but Flutter understood everything.

Now, for a long time, Wise Wit had been missing

one eye. Strange rumors went about that he had lost his eye in the well of wisdom. Flutter was disturbed about it, but not because Wise Wit couldn't manage with only one eye. He could cope very well, but his character had changed. And, seriously, a raven ought to have two eyes—certainly a raven like Wise Wit.

Because each eye had a different kind of vision.

One was a daytime eye. With this he saw the sun, and everything was colored by the sun. He saw the light and the bright, warm colors. He saw the joy in life, the smiles and laughter, the cheerful thoughts, the good. That eye also looked far into the future, and saw what would happen.

But the other eye was a night eye that saw everything colored by the moon. The dark and cold colors. He saw with this the clouds and sorrow; the grim, bleak thoughts, the ugly and the evil. And that eye looked back in time: it could focus far, far back into the past.

Wise Wit had lost his nighttime eye, the moon eye, the primeval eye. The bad eye, as it was called. And it certainly had changed him. Now he saw life only in rosy colors. He could grasp only the happy and the good. And he couldn't see a single shadow any more. He didn't even see his own shadow. The question is whether, at one time, he even couldn't see himself, since he was so black. All this had made him a trifle lighthearted. It wasn't exactly suitable for a raven, but naturally he couldn't be held responsible. Flutter understood that.

And, indeed, she also thought luck could be found even in bad luck, for at least he had not lost his good eye. Then the whole of life would have looked black to him. But on the other hand, she wondered if Wise Wit really was the proper name for him now.

It is beautiful, of course, to be able to see the day-side of life, truly it is, but those who tell the real truth are those who can see the shadowy side too.

And, in fact, she thought that Wise Wit had become a bit superficial.

3

NOW IT WAS time for the autumn fair in Blekeryd, and the roads were crowded with folk. Many came from far away in wagons; others walked or pushed and pulled their loaded carts.

Wandering gypsies came, splendid to see, gay with windblown curls and shining eyes. Foreign voices echoed along the roads where they passed with their music and playfulness; their bright skirts flashed, and their jewelry twinkled.

Watching them pass, everyone was seized with excitement.

Sofia sat next to Albert on the driver's seat, with Klara between them, holding Klas on her lap. They drove slowly and enjoyed the ride.

The morning was clear and soft. Sunlight slipped between the tops of the pines, bringing little warmth for it was autumn. Thistle down drifted over the road and made the air mysteriously silver.

Albert and Sofia smiled at each other, and the children laughed.

At the market place, Albert had rented a shop with a shingle roof. He shared it, as usual, with another glassblower. There he arranged his glassware. It was more beautiful than the other man's, but that didn't help very much, for the other was a better salesman, good at talking, and already busy selling.

And so it went as usual: people looked a long time at Albert's glassware, but bought from his neighbor. It seemed as though fate were against him, and Albert came near to losing hope and courage. Sofia, who had been so full of expectation all morning, grew even paler.

What was the point of striving so hard, of making the most beautiful crystal, if no one wanted it?

Why couldn't Albert make glass that people wanted?

How would they ever manage?

They'd had to borrow the wagon and they'd had to hire the shop for a lot of money. And so far he hadn't sold a single glass. No one even wanted to make an exchange. The day passed.

It was already well into the afternoon. They couldn't afford to stay overnight. They had to start on their way home with their mission unaccomplished.

The children began to grow fretful. Klara, who had run around the streets of the fairground playing with other children, now sat behind the shop with Klas. They were warm enough with a rug over them and they didn't really need anything, but their parents' anxiety affected them, too. They followed everything that happened with big eyes and they looked scared.

Then, suddenly, everything changed.

A man came walking down the market street. He was a nobleman, everything indicated that: his clothes, his walk, his gestures. And he had an old coachman who cleared the way for him through the throngs of people. They walked slowly and spoke to no one. And they had bought nothing.

But then they came to Albert the glassblower's shop. The coachman had already passed by when the nobleman stopped and called to him. He had a cane, and now he began to point to one glass object after another. Then he nodded, gestured, and gave a curt order to the coachman, who immediately walked up to Albert and asked to buy what his lordship wanted.

Meanwhile, the nobleman stared at Klas and Klara. He was rather a young man, but his face was without joy. He looked thoughtfully at the children, but he didn't smile for an instant.

The coachman paid with great shiny coins, a whole handful, and when Albert wanted to give some back, his lordship waved his hand apologetically, then walked away. Without knowing it, the nobleman had done a good deed. But he had not exchanged a single word with Albert.

What did Albert care about that? They were saved now! In a short while they had sold more than they had ever dreamed they could.

They looked at each other, and Albert felt giddy with good fortune.

Now to have some fun!

They would close the shop for the day and move into the inn. There they would put the children to bed and then return to the fairground and join in the merriment. They could actually afford to do it this once! It didn't happen that often. . . .

Could Albert really mean what he said? Sofia hesitated, doubtful, but the roses rushed to bloom in her cheeks.

"Do you think we can get a room in the inn?" she asked.

"Go right now and take the children with you," suggested Albert. "I'll arrange everything here and follow in a little while."

It was already dusk. Lamps were lit in the shops and stalls, and grand torches flamed and flickered in the market square.

Right in the midst of the milling crowd filling the market street stood Albert and Sofia. Now they were content and free to do whatever they pleased, and so Albert said to Sofia, "You shall have a gift from me, Sofia, from this fair."

"Oh no," protested Sofia, blushing.

"Yes," said Albert.

But first they had to buy something for the children who were sleeping in the inn. And so they bought caramels and wooden shoes for both of them and a wooden horse for Klas and a little cloth doll for Klara. The doll wore a blouse and skirt, with an apron and a kerchief around her head.

But what should they buy for Sofia? What did she want? She didn't know right off. . . . A shawl with roses on it?

No, her old one was good enough. It ought to be something she didn't already have.

A little bottle of perfume, perhaps? That should be just the thing, thought Albert.

"Oh no, that's silly," laughed Sofia.

Well, then, he didn't know. . . .

A little old man, a really old man, very little and wizen, sat in a stall selling jewelry. He didn't have much to sell and his stall was a little out of the way.

Albert and Sofia had passed by there several times without stopping. The old man had no lantern, and the place was so murky that they didn't notice him.

But just then the moon rose and flooded the old man and his stall with the clearest light. The next time Albert and Sofia passed, they saw him holding out a ring.

"Would you like a ring?" asked Albert, walking toward the stall.

Sofia caught up with him. A ring. . . .

"It would be too expensive, Albert, dear."

Part One

The old man stood there motionless. He was terribly little, almost a dwarf, really troll-like. His eyes were like lumps of coal in his face, while his hair and beard bristled and shone white in the moonlight. He said nothing, just held out the ring.

Sofia's glance fell on it. And immediately it was as if she had always wanted that very ring and had never known it before. She was seized with desire for it, and Albert saw this.

"We can at least hear what it costs," he said.

This sent a shiver through Sofia. She was a little afraid of the old man, but she followed Albert toward him.

The old man didn't answer Albert's question about the price. He took Sofia's hand and slipped the ring on her trembling finger. It fitted perfectly.

Mounted in a heavy silver setting, a dark, iridescent green stone glowed bewitchingly. Sofia stood very still, one hand holding the other, which wore the ring. Albert asked her a question, but she couldn't seem to say anything. She stood there in the moonlight, and her glance was drawn deeper and deeper into the stone's glittering depth, as though into an eye. She felt as if it were looking back at her. Time stood still.

Now Albert asked again, "Would you like it?" He sounded happy. He had arranged a price meanwhile with the old man. They could afford the ring.

"Thank you, Albert," sighed Sofia in answer.

And so she could keep the ring. Albert paid and they walked away. They had no more errands to do, but they walked around the fairground and enjoyed themselves.

The next time they passed the spot where the old man had been, he had gone, both he and his stall. And the moon had slipped behind the forest. The place where he had stood was now like a dark hole.

A strange fear made Sofia shudder. Quickly she turned and drew Albert back toward the festive square.

4

FLUTTER MILDWEATHER had come to the fair as usual and set up her fortune-telling tent. She'd brought along several carpets in both light and dark colors and they hung outside on a rack.

On this occasion, Wise Wit, her raven, sat in a cage. It was an old, gilded cage that she'd hung from a hook in the top of the tent. When people entered the tent and happened to brush against the cage, it would begin to rock. That startled Wise Wit, and he would come out with the words:

"I am Wise Wit, the black raven, whose answers are more truthful than people's questions."

Some people grew angry when they heard this and thought the raven was boasting; others felt he was amusing, but most were overcome with awe.

But Flutter Mildweather didn't really like his behavior, which she thought undignified. In ordinary circumstances he wouldn't have described himself that way—it had something to do with his having only one eye. And she told him so, that he wasn't as wise as he thought; on the contrary, his way of seeing things and people was rather superficial and silly.

But the raven didn't agree. He answered calmly, "The wise are seldom happy. Moderately wise is what one should be."

Then Flutter sighed, for there was truth in his words—it was what she, herself, experienced every day. She paced the tent again and again, staring anxiously at the pattern in the carpet she had finished just in time for the fair. Every glance left her equally upset and unhappy. Her steps were heavy and, when she shook her head, the flowers and butterfly wings on her hat bobbed and swayed mournfully.

Wise Wit turned his eye to her:

"There's better advice than dread and lament," he said reprovingly.

"Yes, indeed, Wise Wit," she had to answer truthfully. "But then what advice would you give?"

"So you've seen some dreadful unhappiness in the carpet again?" asked the raven.

She nodded silently.

"I saw that, and I've held my tongue about it," said Wise Wit, very determined.

"But if she comes and asks me to tell her fortune?"

"I'm shutting my mouth," answered Wise Wit, and he blinked his eye wisely.

Part One

The whole fairground was bathed in moonlight, and the sky clustered full of stars. Now and then a shooting star fell and people got to wish for what they wanted.

"I want us to become rich!" Sofia wished.

But Albert didn't wish anything for himself. He felt they'd already received so much that day.

"I mean for the children's sake," Sofia added. "I want them to have a better life than ours."

"Things are fine for us," said Albert quietly.

But Sofia didn't listen to him. Just as a star fell she said, "Think how sweet Klara would look in silk and Klas in satin—I want that for them!" She whispered it, and her eyes glittered, dreaming in the moonlight.

They came to Flutter Mildweather's fortune-telling tent, and Albert stopped to look at the carpets hanging there. He stood there a long while thinking about them. He saw they were more beautiful than ever before, but in a darker and more mysterious way. And he felt a strange, heart-sickening gloom as he stood there, as if struck by a foreboding of unhappiness.

Flutter Mildweather herself was nowhere to be seen. The raven Wise Wit perched dead still in his cage. Albert turned to Sofia. He wondered if she felt as he did, especially about one particular carpet, which filled him with melancholy and sorrow.

But Sofia wasn't looking at the carpets at all, nor

was she listening to the musicians playing dance music at the crossroads.

She did a little dance step and smiled.

"I think I'll have my fortune told, Albert," she announced.

"Wouldn't you like to dance?" asked Albert, who wanted to get away from there.

"Later. When I've heard my fortune."

And so Sofia stepped into the tent. Wise Wit saw her but made nary a sound. There inside sat Flutter Mildweather on a three-legged stool. One of her marvelous carpets covered the floor. Sofia didn't like them, for they were too gloomy and dark.

Flutter wore her hat, and the brim hid her face. Her shoulder cape drooped. She was staring at the floor and didn't look up when Sofia entered.

"I want to have my fortune told," said Sofia.

"I've finished telling fortunes for today," Flutter answered curtly.

"Oh," said Sofia, disappointed, "I did so want to...."

The mint-blue eyes wandered a moment over Sofia's face and then looked away.

"That doesn't make any difference," said Flutter, "and besides, you don't know what you want."

Then Sofia became angry. She thought Flutter was acting that way just because they came from the same village. Of course Flutter didn't feel she had to bow and scrape to people from home, but Sofia wouldn't give up. Stubbornly, she stretched out her hand.

"Look at it! Tell my fortune now!" she demanded. At first Flutter tried to act as if she didn't see it. Then she looked at it, suddenly staring at the ring Sofia was wearing. Finally she closed her eyes and shook her head.

"No!" she said. "No and again no!"

Sofia let her hand fall to her side. She was sad and offended. She wanted to put out her hand again, but couldn't find the right words to express her indignation. But Flutter understood, nevertheless. Once more she fastened those elusive blue eyes on her and whispered,

"Dear child"—that was all she said—"dear child...."

Then Sofia looked down and realized that she'd

been wrong: Flutter really was very tired. Sofia felt a little ashamed of herself and turned back toward the door. Behind her she heard Flutter say in a gentle voice,

"You're wearing a ring, Sofia. If misfortune should ever befall you one day, you must send me that ring, and I'll help you, wherever you may be. Don't forget my words! Send me the ring!"

Sofia stopped while Flutter spoke. She stood just under Wise Wit's cage. The raven had fallen asleep; his eyes were closed.

Sofia didn't feel like dancing at all after that. She told Albert everything.

"She wanted my ring, can you imagine!" she burst out indignantly.

"That's not really the point," said Albert, for Flutter hadn't behaved at all like herself. "I think I'll let her tell my fortune, and then we'll see. After all, I don't have a ring."

He walked into the tent, and he stayed in there a long time. Meanwhile Sofia wandered off to listen to the music. She came back just as Albert was leaving the tent. He took big long steps as if he were in a terrible hurry.

And the raven, Wise Wit, woke and called after him in his hoarse voice, "Believe it if you want to! It's all the same to me."

"What is it, Albert?" Sofia asked, terrified.

"Come on!" he cried, drawing her along with him. He almost ran with her.

"Did she tell your fortune?"

He didn't answer.

"Albert?"

But he only made her hurry all the faster. Finally Sofia asked no more questions. She just ran silently and obediently by his side.

When they came to the inn, Albert burst open the door to the little room they had rented. Without a word he rushed over to the sofa where the children lay. He looked quite wild with frenzy. Leaning over them, he whispered several times,

"Thank God, thank God. . . ."

They lay there, sleeping so sweetly. Sofia looked at him anxiously.

"What came over you? Did you think the children had disappeared?"

But Albert would not answer her question directly. He said he was tired and wanted to go straight to bed. It was just something he had on his mind, he said. It must have been the raven and the moonlight and those carpets. . . .

"Yes indeed," agreed Sofia. "Somehow those carpets are horrible."

They laid the doll next to Klara, and the wooden horse beside Klas, and then they went to bed. But Albert lay awake for a long while, twisting and turning.

The room had no window, only a little louver through which the moonlight slipped in. It cut through the darkness mercilessly, cold and blue, until Sofia rose up from their bed and covered the louver with her skirt.

In the pale light before dawn Albert rose and packed their wagon. They left Blekeryd before the sun rose on a new day.

5

A CHANGE HAD come over Albert.

He stayed at home much more than before and after nightfall he never returned to the workshop.

It was as though he was afraid of something. He was obviously anxious about locking the door and closing the window properly. At the slightest unusual sound he'd jump up to see what it was, and if the children were out of sight he almost lost his mind with fear.

Sometimes he came over from the workshop in the middle of a clear bright morning just to see if everything was all right.

But if Sofia were to ask what was worrying him, he would avoid answering by saying that any number of unknown dangers always threatened little children, that you could never be vigilant enough, never careful enough about them.

Sofia knew that this anxiety had come upon him after the autumn fair. But what had happened there, in fact? Well, he'd been to see Flutter Mildweather and she had told his fortune. Could something the old lady said have scared him? He insisted that she hadn't said anything special. She'd only rambled on the way old crones telling fortunes always do, he said. He couldn't even remember exactly what she'd told him. And, in any case, he wasn't the kind of person who worried about the fortune-telling prattle of old women.

That was what Albert said, but then why did he behave so strangely? Sofia got no answer to so many questions, and at last she wearied of asking.

Whether or not she had caught Albert's anxiety, she herself felt far from content, even though she'd been given such a fine ring. How could she be so ungrateful? Sometimes she wished she hadn't accepted it. It was such an inappropriate present for her! They should have bought something more sensible with the money.

Whenever she put the ring on her finger, she was filled with alarm. It was just as well that she wasn't used to finery: such showing off wasn't for poor people. The thought that the children might have got something warm for the winter instead weighed heavily on her conscience.

She was sure that this was what made her so uneasy and upset every time she wore the ring. One day she could bear it no longer. She took the ring off her finger and hid it so as not to wear it ever again. Then everything became easier. And Albert didn't notice a thing.

Part One

Now, once again, Sofia went from farm to farm as usual, beating the harvested flax. Luckily she found this work to do, for Albert wasn't able to make very much glass that autumn. And they had next to nothing saved up to fall back on.

That winter turned out to be long and cold and grey, but then, finally, spring came and it seemed as if everything eased up all at once.

When everything in nature turned lighter and brighter, Albert began to be his cheerful old self again. For even he couldn't resist the spring. He got on much faster with his glass in the workshop—for indeed his work had slowed down throughout the winter—and now he had to make enough glass to sell in the spring fair.

This time he wanted to travel to the fair alone. There was no changing his mind. The children were too young to come along, they'd been such a worry the last time. Sofia was disappointed, but there was nothing to be done about it. She resigned herself to staying at home.

Albert arranged to travel with a farmer who carved wooden clogs and other wooden articles. This time Albert had just enough glassware to fit in easily with the farmer's own load.

He would stay over night in Blekeryd and travel back the following morning with the farmer. They planned to be back early.

But for Sofia, waiting at home, it proved to be an endless day. They didn't come when they had promised. Sofia must have run to the crossroad a hundred times to see if they were coming.

In the end she grew angry and anxious, and then she forgot to keep an eye on the children, though that had been her last promise to Albert.

Not that Klas and Klara needed anything. Klas had learned to walk during the winter and was really steady on his feet now. And Klara was grown up for her age.

She took Klas by the hand and they walked out along the lane to watch their mother run down to the big road. Sofia had told them to stay in the cottage, but why should they do that? It was so beautiful outside. The sun was shining and all the birds singing. Green had returned to the grass. And look, there far down the lane you could see mother walking. They followed her until she disappeared around a bend.

And then they met two girls who explained how they could make a good deal of money that day from passersby homeward bound from the fair. All you had to do was walk into the forest and pick wild flowers, and then stand down near the big road where the carriages and wagons passed. You just waved the flowers and then people would stop and buy them, because everyone had a lot of money that day.

What a good idea! Father and mother always had so little money. Where could they find flowers?

The girls knew that, too. They could show them. The forest was full of flowers. All kinds bloomed in there.

White and blue anemones?

Yes, lots of them.

And so the girls led the way. Klas and Klara followed them. It was just as they said. The forest fairly glowed with blue and white anemones, everywhere. They picked big bunches, all together.

They didn't need to wander very far into the forest. There was no danger of getting lost, as mother and father were always so afraid might happen. The girls knew their way perfectly.

Later they took a shortcut through the forest down to the big road. And there was a sight to behold! Many children already lined the route, all waving bouquets at the travelers as they passed.

The happy farmers homeward bound were free and generous with their earnings. They often bought several bouquets, but perhaps Klas and Klara were too little or perhaps they didn't wave their flowers as prettily as the others did, because no one bought from them.

Soon the girls had sold all their flowers, and ran off into the forest to gather some more.

Klas and Klara wandered a little further down the road to see if they couldn't do better there. Klas' arms grew tired and he dropped blossoms along the way. The little flowers began to droop and wilt, too.

But still they stood there waiting patiently. They weren't particularly well dressed. In fact, they looked like little bundles of clothes out of which stuck tufts of hair. Their round mouths gaped and their blue eyes peeped out full of longing. They looked rather funny standing there, waiting for a miracle.

And the miracle came at last.

A fine carriage rumbled along, not one of the common kind farmers have with sturdy, stocky, slow horses, but a beautiful coach drawn by two sleek white horses, with a coachman on the driver's seat. The horses galloped so fast that a white cloud of dust haloed each hoof and their manes streamed gloriously.

Now, this carriage had windows with curtains and, just as the carriage drove past Klas and Klara, someone inside waved.

A little further on the coachman reined in the horses and the coach came to a stop right in the middle of the road. The coachman got down and opened the door.

A crowd of children rushed over and collected around the coach right away, but the coachman drove them off. He beckoned instead to Klas and Klara. Can you imagine, he wanted their flowers!

Inside the coach sat a fine couple, a beautiful lady and a noble gentleman. They smiled at the solemn little children who stood there staring open-mouthed. The man, especially, smiled at the two of them. He said he recognized them; he had bought crystal from their father at the Blekeryd fair last autumn. Did they remember?

No, they didn't. But he wanted their flowers, anyway. He said something to the coachman, who took out a big coin and gave it to Klara, and then the rich man told him to give one to Klas, too.

They were so astonished that they forgot to hand over their flowers, and the coachman had to tell them to give them to the fine lady.

The lady took them and laid them beside her on the seat. She scarcely glanced at them, but the nobleman said they were beautiful. And then he smiled again at Klas and Klara and asked the lady if she didn't agree that the children were sweet.

"Yes," she answered, "very pretty. Shall we drive on now?"

"As you wish, my dear," he said, and nodded to the children. The coachman closed the door. He was really old, and before he clambered back up onto the box, he looked sternly at the children and told them gruffly not to lose the coins but to go right home and give them to their father and mother.

"Because that is a lot of money," he explained very seriously.

The coach started off; a pale, pretty hand waved sadly through the curtains; the nobleman's face could be seen briefly; but then the horses pulled away so swiftly that the coach disappeared in a cloud of dust.

Klas and Klara stood speechless, gaping after it. Almost immediately all the children surrounded them to see the coins. And surely they would have lost them very soon if Sofia hadn't come running over that same instant. She was white with fright.

Her feelings changed to astonishment when she saw what the children had been given. Astonishment and delight.

"Real gold coins!" she told them.

They walked home to wait for Albert, but now Sofia didn't dare run down to the crossroad any more. She stayed very watchfully inside.

The day ended and night came. Still no Albert. He wasn't home until after ten o'clock.

By then the children were fast asleep in the chest of drawers.

He had been delayed by an unexpected misfortune: The farmer had, of course, got quite drunk at the fair and had driven like a madman, so that on their way home the wagon had rolled straight into a ditch. Every single glass had been smashed, but that didn't make much difference, since no one wanted his work anyway. He hadn't been able to sell a single piece. As usual!

No rich folk had come to buy from him this time, either. Albert was depressed and fed up with everything.

Sofia looked as if she were bursting with secrets, but said nothing. Then, when he had finished telling her what had happened, she took out the gold coins that the children had received and showed them to him.

"Wealthy folk have been here, and that's for sure," she said.

Albert's eyes opened very wide.

"But you had nothing to sell," he exclaimed.

"I didn't," she laughed, "but the children did. They gathered flowers and sold them down by the road."

Then she told about the fine coach with the noble couple who wanted to buy only from their children, not from the others. Sofia was so proud, but Albert frowned. He wasn't as happy about the story as she.

In the first place, he didn't like the fact that she had left the children unattended.

And then it was bitter for him to realize that a handful of wilting flowers could be worth more than his glass. What was it all worth, his glassblowing?

And so ended the fair that spring.

6

A SUMMER CAME and went, and then a winter, too, and thus the spring of a new year returned.

Albert and Sofia watched the seasons change and their children grow bigger, but otherwise everything stayed much the same. Their life plodded along the same old ruts.

Whether it earned him money or not, Albert had to keep making his glass, for while he worked he was always happy. Nor did he worry whether the pieces would sell or not. When at work he forgot everything else and felt content.

How he longed to be able to stay in his workshop and avoid going to the fairs! But they were in fact his only way to sell, for in the village few people ever needed glass, and no one could make a living selling there.

But as for Sofia, she always looked forward to each and every fair. She lived for them. And this spring he'd promised that she could come along. The children were so much bigger now. And the fair at Blekeryd came later this year than usual, at the end of May, so that they could count on fine, warm weather.

At each fair Sofia always thought Albert would have great success. Someday it just had to work out for them, she thought. Some time it had to be their turn for good luck. Why not this next fair? Yes, at every fair she felt sure that now, NOW it was going to happen! Albert would sell all his glasses and every one of his bowls.

She boosted Albert's confidence this way as they packed the wagon full of glass, until at last he, too, was all afire with hope. When they set off that beautiful May morning, they were full of joy and expectation.

It was also a marvelous day. The wild cherry trees were just at the peak of their bloom, spreading their scent afar, and the dandelion seeds sailed through the sunlight over the fairground. On such a day as this, surely all would go well.

It looked as if everyone thought the same. An uncommonly large crowd had gathered, and the fair offered more amusements than usual. One man had put up a Punch-and-Judy theatre. A real carousel had come, and in one tent a snake charmer and several sword-swallowers performed. One organ grinder had brought a bear with him, and another a monkey.

44

Many more children had been allowed to come along, too. The gypsies, of course, always had their lovely children with them, but other children showed up. The place was alive with them, echoing with joyful shouts.

When Sofia saw this she told Albert it was good that Klas and Klara could come, for they really needed a little entertainment. Of course Albert agreed.

There was so much for the children to see.

Especially wonderful was a shop with dolls. An old woman had made all the dolls herself. They sat and stood on shelves or hung from the roof beams by lengths of string. They were large, almost like little children, and had the most delightful blue button eyes and curly hair. The clothes were so realistic and well-made that everyone who saw them marveled.

There was always a crowd around that shop, both mothers and daughters, touching the clothes and stroking the dolls' heads and sighing with delight. But not everyone could buy them because the dolls were expensive. Most people had to wait and see how their own sales went before they could think about buying a doll. Only rich people from the city could buy them right away.

Sofia and Klara had already been over to the doll shop several times to see which doll they liked the most. They picked out one of the largest, most expensive ones, and neither of them seriously believed

that the doll would ever be theirs, but it didn't cost anything to wish. Her blond hair was braided in long golden plaits; she wore a black satin cloak and a lilac kerchief. You couldn't describe how pretty she was.

Every time Sofia took Klara with her to look at the doll, both of them worried just as much that she might already be sold and gone. But imagine, she still hung there in her corner, swinging from a little string. It was exactly as if she were waiting for them, they thought.

And then, when Albert actually sold a pair of goblets, Klara's hopes became more real. And Sofia's, too. Perhaps after all . . .

Of course the other glassblower with whom Albert shared the shop sold the most as usual, but he didn't have as much with him this time. And people felt in a fine mood because of the sunshine. They were eager to buy.

The other man had already sold out before the morning was over, and so people started coming to Albert instead. It went really well, and soon Sofia had to help him.

Because of this she couldn't keep an eye on the children all the time, but she told them to stay nearby. And they did, too. They behaved very well in the beginning. But then Klara decided she had to go over and see the doll again.

She wandered off with Klas. Of course she knew

the way, because she and her mother had walked it so often. But how much there was to look at everywhere! And what a crush of people running this way and that! Swept up in the rush, the children began to run hither and thither like everyone else.

And every now and then some gypsy children came up to them, and they would play together for a while. And then they'd set off again, and they walked . . . and walked . . . and walked. . . .

Suddenly Sofia noticed that the children didn't answer when she called. She ran out of the shop. They were nowhere to be seen. She asked the shopkeepers nearby. They knew nothing. But what danger could there be, they said. The children would be all right. Why shouldn't they look around a little?

On such a blessed day no one need be afraid!

No, that was the truth! Sofia wasn't exactly frightened, either, but she told Albert that he would have to manage alone for a while because she had to look after the children. She didn't want to tell him what had happened because that would have upset him needlessly. When she thought about it, Sofia realized that Klara must have wandered off toward the doll shop.

Sofia hurried over there. As usual it was crowded with people, but her children were not among them. She described them and asked if anyone had seen them. No, they hadn't shown up, at least not recently.

In that case they must be on their way back, Sofia decided, and hurried off. But then she thought that as long as she was there, she'd see if the doll with the satin cloak was still for sale. They might be able to buy it after all, if they could keep on selling so well all day.

But the doll was gone.

And then her spirits fell very low indeed. Poor little Klara, such a disappointment for her. Sofia just had to ask if the doll was really sold or if perhaps it had been taken down from view. She pushed her way through the crowd up to the old woman.

Yes, indeed, the doll was really sold.

"Oh, alas, what a shame! I wonder who bought it?" Sofia asked, mostly to herself. But then what a strange answer she heard!

The old lady told her that a little girl had come and bought the doll. And in her opinion it was outrageous that little children should be allowed to buy such expensive things by themselves. The little girl wasn't with an adult, only her little brother. It really was the limit, said the old lady, to send children out with so much money. . . .

Sofia, seized by a terrible foreboding, asked what the children looked like. From the description, there was no doubt about it: they were Klas and Klara. She was absolutely terrified. Where in heavens had they got the money?

She asked the lady in what direction they'd walked away, but she didn't know. She'd only noticed how blissfully happy the little girl looked setting off with the big doll in her arms and her little brother trailing along after her.

How long ago could that have been? The old lady thought it must have been a good hour at least.

Her heart pounding with fear, Sofia ran back to the shop. Perhaps the children had already returned. Of course they must have lost their way for a while. It wouldn't be easy for them to see their way through the crowd of tall, bustling people.

But there were no children back with Albert. He hadn't seen them. He turned pale and panic-stricken when Sofia told him about what had happened. He dropped what he was doing and rushed off to search for them.

Now the fairground was really very large. They could have wandered far afield. And surely not everyone there was nice and kind, Albert said. You could never really know what strange people might come to a fairground.

Sofia tried to calm Albert.

It was truly such a wonderful day. Everyone would be nice and happy. No one could want to harm two small children, he must believe that!

Albert didn't answer. His face tense with effort, he searched on and on, relentlessly. He asked everyone. They all gave him the same answer, that the place was crawling with children. How could you be sure which ones you'd seen? But they promised to keep a look out. There really wasn't any danger. Think how playful children run off for a while and hide.

But the hours passed and the day sank slowly into dusk. Albert and Sofia had abandoned their glassware completely. And this was the one time they had been able to sell. Surely they had boasted . . . been over-proud. . . .

They searched, wandering like lost souls. And others helped them, too, now that they understood it was serious. For no children playing a game would hide so long. If nothing else, they would surely become hungry and thirsty.

Finally they had searched through all the wagons left in the woods around the edge of the fairground. Perhaps the children had lost their way there, become tired, crept inside one of the wagons, and fallen asleep.

But they weren't there, either.

They had disappeared without a trace.

At the doll shop the trail just ended. Afterward not a single person had seen them.

The day had been warm, but now evening brought a refreshing coolness. The moon rose, big and pale and bright. And the shimmering blue air was filled with song and the sounds of games and laughter. But neither Albert nor Sofia saw or heard what was happening around them any longer.

Sofia was beside herself. She stumbled on by Albert's side, and once an accident almost happened. She tripped and fell right in front of a big, elegant coach, slowly easing its way through the pleasure-seekers. It was a black, closed carriage, drawn by two horses. Curtains in the coach windows were elegantly drawn. Curious eyes watched the coach pass by.

People staring after it would have been astonished had they known that behind the curtains two lonely children slumbered in each other's arms. A large fairground doll had slipped out of the girl's lap and fallen to the floor of the coach.

And this was the coach that nearly ran over Sofia. The man on the driver's seat reined in the horses instantly. They reared. Albert grabbed hold of Sofia and pulled her toward him. The coachman glanced blankly at the crying woman who hadn't looked where she was going. Then, urging the horses on, he drove off, finally clear of the crowd in the fairground streets.

The last he saw was an eccentrically dressed old lady who suddenly appeared from the shadows mottling the moonlight and fluttered a little way ahead of the coach. She wore a cloak with a big floppy collar and looked just like an old bird.

When the coachman drove past her, she looked straight at him, so penetratingly that he became weirdly frightened. She held her ground and stared at the coach until it swung away around a bend in

the road and disappeared from her sight. This was a
relief to the coachman. He had felt her eyes staring
at him the whole time.

They traveled all through the night. Northward.
No one knew what roads they took.

The forests stood dark and silent, so that one
could hear the wood nixie sing. She was dangerous,

the wood nixie, especially for young men. But the coachman looked neither to the right nor the left, for he was old and didn't let himself be enticed.

They drove along moonwhite roads, between fields, with clumps of moss and anthills, where will-o'-the-wisps danced with their lights. They rode until the moon paled away and the air began to murmur with small blusters of wind. Morning came, and still they drove. White butterflies fluttered over the road.

They drove through the night and the day, and the whole time the children slept quietly on within the coach. . . .

Part
Two

"Those who know nothing
never know
that many are lulled by success,
one man is rich,
another poor,
but that never counts in the reckoning."

HAVAMAL

7

THE HOUSE STOOD in a most remarkable town. All Wishes Town it was called—but it doesn't exist any more.

It was encircled by a high wall, with battlements, turrets, and towers, and was also surrounded by water, for it lay on an island in the River of Forgotten Memories. It was said to be unapproachable.

The deserted streets stretched out their grey cobblestones and black rows of street lamps. They met at intersections, crisscrossed, went on, but where houses should be there was nothing. There were no other houses, only the one.

Every evening the street lamps were lit, but no one walked about, for those who lived in the House seldom went out, and if they did, they drove off in a coach.

It was a dark stone house, high, and mighty in its loneliness, a gloomy sight to see.

Now, the man who founded All Wishes Town had

been full of grand fancies. He wanted to do so much that it took him his whole lifetime just to mull over his dreams. He gave the town its name, and nothing more. His son built the House and laid out the streets, but then that was the end of him, too. He had to leave the rest of it to his descendants.

One of them was the Lord who lived there now, and the street lamps were his contribution. At that time few cities had street lighting, so it was very special.

But he had something else to think about.

For it so happened that his wife, the Lady, was very, very unhappy.

She had everything: beauty, wealth, power. Her husband fulfilled her slightest wish. She need never be alone, because, even if there weren't any people in the town, many lived in the countryside nearby. But she didn't want to see anyone; she kept to herself.

Those who didn't like her said she acted this way only to make herself seem interesting. But that was not true, for she was actually in deep despair.

Everyone pitied the Lord, who was so nice and devoted and self-sacrificing. He was always rushing over to her and asking her anxiously what she would like. And what did he get as an answer?

Well, something like this:

"What good does it do to wish when all your wishes come true?"

Part Two

Or:

"Don't you see that you're stealing my wishes, when you bring all your gifts?"

No, that was something the Lord could not understand. And no one else did, either. People hastily made the sign of the cross and felt they had reason to doubt her sanity.

The Lord of All Wishes Town was a young and handsome man, and he knew that. He had been born rich and powerful. He had no one to be grateful to for anything in the world, because everything had been his from the beginning.

He loved to make people happy, to give presents and fulfill wishes. He'd always done just that, for he also had been born good and kind.

What a great pleasure he had experienced when he first met the poor young girl dressed in rags who owned nothing in the world. What joy was his to be able to make her the Lady of the House in All Wishes Town.

This was a joy that would never end.

She who had owned nothing and had been nothing from the first—through her he would experience this joy again and again and again.

He only asked of her that she always have a wish in readiness for him. A wish he could fulfill.

A simple enough request, as you can see; she could certainly oblige him.

But instead she acted strangely; she retired into

herself, announcing that she had no further wishes. They had all been stolen from her, she said.

Now, there was one word the Lord loved above all others.

It was the little word "thanks."

An unusual word. For though in his ears it had a lovely, soothing sound, in his mouth it had an unpleasant taste. He had tried it out, so he knew.

Once the Lady had embroidered a pair of slippers as a present for him, and when she gave them to him, she said, "How would it be for you to say thank you?"

At first he didn't understand what she meant, and laughed at her. Should he be the one. . . ? Surely she was joking?

But she wasn't. She was determined. She said he really ought to try it, so he'd know how it felt.

And of course he'd do it, if it would make her happy.

But the word lay there like a lump in his mouth, and he didn't think he'd ever be able to get it out. In the end there was nothing for him to do but spit it out.

The Lady insisted that it hit her right in the face. But why, after all, should she force him? She could clearly see that it was hard for him, because he'd never had any reason to use the word. Naturally it was easier for others.

He didn't stop loving to hear that little word because of this. On the contrary, he noticed his craving for it increased more rapidly after that.

But he was on his guard in the future in case he might have to receive gifts or services from the Lady.

He was such a calm and reliable and prudent man. He never forgot himself. If only she would express a wish, then everything would be fine.

But she refused.

One single wish was all she had expressed.

"I would like children," she said once. "I would like to present you with a son." That was what she said. *Present* you, she said, and then he understood that she wanted to get him to have to say thank you again.

He didn't let himself be trapped; he was too smart for that. But the matter worried him greatly nevertheless. She had expressed a wish and he was obliged to fulfill it.

She must have her child. Either a son or one of each, for that matter. Naturally it wasn't impossible, but still it was a problem. He had to mull it over for a long while.

Then, gradually, an image began to grow and take shape in his mind.

At the Blekeryd fair he'd seen two small children who had won his heart. That was a couple of years ago. But then he had caught sight of them again last spring when he and the Lady had driven through

Nöda village. They had been standing by the road-
side selling anemones, and he had bought their
flowers. Just that once the Lady had allowed herself
a faint smile, and she had said they were sweet. She
had definitely liked them.

So there they were, the children he was looking
for. A boy and a girl!

The Lord was not an evil man; on the contrary,
everyone could vouch for his goodness. But he was
blinded. He only saw what he wanted to see.

He pictured before him the glassblower and his
children. He didn't see the glassblower's wife at all.

He imagined for himself how poor a glassblower
must be. And what a burden it must be to care for
two small children.

It would be such a relief to the poor father if the
Lord would just take in his starving little ones. He
would give them a bright future.

And then some day the father would thank him,
even though perhaps he wouldn't understand right
from the start that it was for their own good. Unfor-
tunately you have to expect that kind of
misunderstanding.

Therefore the father shouldn't know anything
about it, at least not right away. It would be better
to get hold of the children first so that he could
get used to the idea of their being gone.

Then, slowly, one could tell him. Or one might
send him a sum of money as consolation. But there

was no hurry about that. First the man would have to calm down and appreciate how good the new arrangement was.

Yes indeed, it was a superb plan.

The more the Lord thought about it, the better it seemed to him. And the children were absolutely delightful. They were obviously not spoiled. Wasn't that a wonderful advantage to start with?

The Lady wouldn't be plagued by the children screaming and shouting, she who suffered headaches so easily.

Personally, he thought older children were much more fun, because they could actually *understand* what he was doing for them. They'd be old enough to say thank you.

The thought made him very cheerful, and so, content with his plans, he went out and gave his coachman the order to drive to Blekeryd.

And that was what lay behind the disappearance of Klas and Klara.

8

TIME PASSED.

Klas and Klara lived in All Wishes Town now, and the House was their home.

They weren't the same children they had been the day they disappeared from the Blekeryd fairground. Their lives had been changed. They were rich and noble children now.

They belonged to the Lord and Lady.

They belonged to the House.

They didn't remember anything about their former lives.

They remembered neither Albert nor Sofia; they felt no loss, no longing, because they had forgotten everything that came before this time.

Without their knowing it, the coachman had given them a sleeping potion at the fair so they would sleep throughout the journey.

When they awoke they were lying, each in his own bed, in a big green room. They didn't know where they had come from or where they were. They didn't recognize anything except each other. But they got up and began a new life without asking any questions. You have to know something to be able to ask. And they knew nothing. What was past returned to them only sometimes, briefly, as a bewildering dream, and disappeared equally swiftly.

Klas and Klara were well-brought-up children. Klara always wore silk clothes and her small, stubby blond pigtails had grown into long, beautiful corkscrew curls. Klas was dressed in satin.

They looked exactly as Sofia had once wished they would at the Blekeryd fair long ago, when the shooting stars fell across the sky.

They also had the most wonderful toys in all the world. Klara no longer had to content herself combing out lengths of flax. She had her own dolls with real hair. And Klas owned a very realistic rocking horse.

They got to eat their favorite food until they grew tired of it and had to think up something new. The cook came in every morning to ask what they wanted to eat. It wasn't always easy to tell her.

Finally they were unable to think up any new treats and sat with sorrowful faces eating their old favorites. Soon they had lost all their appetite. Then they started to get thinner. They ate and ate, for they did what they were told, but they grew thinner and thinner, nevertheless. It was a mystery.

The Lord and the Lady were always nice, but didn't bother with them very much. They liked having them, for such a big house could do with a couple of children to decorate it. And besides, children can be very pleasant to look at when they're neat and well brought up. But naturally they shouldn't take up too much space or attention, especially if they're not your own, thought the Lady.

Though they didn't cheer her up as much as the Lord had expected, at least she accepted them. But she always called them the Lord's children, not hers; they were his "find," she used to say.

In the beginning she devoted more time to them. She enjoyed changing the way they wore their hair and choosing new clothes for them. That amused her for a little while. And after she had turned them out the way she liked, she got them to follow after her when she took walks down the long mirror-lined galleries in the House. Sometimes, if the weather was good, they got to walk in the little garden that was laid out like another room right in the middle of the House.

But most of the time they walked in the mirror rooms. There they would go along hand-in-hand, scarcely daring to look right or left, for they were told to be on their best behavior. They kept their eyes anxiously on the Lady, so as not to make a mistake.

Sometimes she'd stop, and then they would stop,

too. She would stand still a moment and gaze thoughtfully into a mirror. But the children would only stare at her, full of eagerness. For sometimes she would turn to them, smile, and say, "Perhaps I do look better with children than with dogs. . . ."

Then she would nod at them and smile again. That meant they could follow her some more. The Lady was so beautiful but looked so sorrowful. They were happy when she smiled and was pleased with them.

Before the children came, she always used to walk

around followed by a pair of big black greyhounds, and that looked very mournful. She never smiled at the greyhounds.

But sometimes she did smile at Klas and Klara, and everything was fine until Klas spilled jam on his lace collar and Klara wrinkled her clothes. Then the Lady suddenly tired of them and told the Lord that, after all, the dogs really complemented her beauty better.

Then she took walks with her big black greyhounds again. They looked so grim and sniffed along the floors with their pointed noses.

Klas and Klara felt unhappy, for they tried so hard to behave perfectly. And the Lord looked so downcast, too, but he said nothing; he never said anything, merely sighed.

Then, for the most part, the children were left alone, and they missed the Lady. Klara especially longed for her. And once she caught herself calling out, "Mother!" She fell silent, wonderingly, for she didn't know where the word came from, nor in fact what it meant.

They had never called the Lady "mother." They never had a chance to say anything unless they had been spoken to first, and then they were expected to keep their answers short. They answered, "Yes, my Lady," or "No, my Lady."

Sometimes the Lord joked with them, and then they could laugh, but never for too long or too loudly, for that would not have been well-behaved. Otherwise they said "thank you" to him most of the time.

The House was filled with long corridors and enormous rooms. They could easily lose their way in all the rooms. There was absolute silence throughout; they could hear only the echo of their footsteps. Then, frightened, they'd start running. They ran, more and more terrified, but you can't run away from your own footsteps.

Sometimes they stumbled upon someone they didn't know. Then, too, they were frightened, even though they knew that everyone belonged to the House, because no one else could enter it.

Everyone always tiptoed silently about, so as not to give the Lady one of her headaches. The children learned to walk silently, too, and then they didn't make such a loud echo.

There were many stairs in the House, so softly and deeply carpeted, that you couldn't hear the faintest footfall. Klas and Klara often walked up and down. On the stairs, they felt a kind of security. They felt they weren't heard and that they disturbed no one. And they weren't in the way. They could walk up and down the stairs for hours. And they played a game there, pretending that the House was a mountain.

Since no other people lived in the town, they had no children to play with, and none were ever invited

to the House. But Klas and Klara didn't mind that, either, for they knew of no other children but each other.

Moreover, they'd had a remarkable experience—several times.

They weren't allowed to walk in the mirror rooms alone. These were locked when the Lady wasn't passing through them. But a number of other mirrors hung around the House.

Part Two

And so it happened that Klas and Klara got to see two small children walking toward them at the end of a corridor. They were overjoyed. They started running, and the children ran, too, until they met. They always met in front of a mirror.

They'd stand there and remarkable things would happen, for when they leaned their foreheads against the mirror, they pressed against the foreheads of two little children on the other side. They could look into their eyes, which were always bright with excitement. They stood there for ages watching each other, and soon Klas and Klara realized that the only children they would ever meet in the House were the Mirrorchildren.

At first they felt less forlorn and abandoned every time they met, as if they shared their fate with these children who said nothing, whom they could never reach and touch.

But then one day surprise and joy had gone from the Mirrorchildren's faces; they saw only sorrow and anxiety, and then Klas and Klara were very much afraid.

They thought they had everything they wanted. They thought everything was just perfect, but now they felt sorry for the Mirrorchildren. They wanted to do something to help them; they longed to share their sorrows. And soon they felt as if they had done just that, without knowing how it had come about.

Then they didn't want to meet them any more,

they avoided them. They wanted to forget those sorrowful faces.

No mirrors hung on the stairs, and so they sought refuge there, where they could play that the House was just a mountain, not a House at all, just an ordinary old mountain on the ground. On the stairs they were always alone. And if they were unhappy, they didn't know it.

Because it was the Mirrorchildren's unknown sorrows that weighed upon them—not their own.

9

THE HOUSE WAS full of servants who took turns looking after the children. But since there were new servants all the time, Klas and Klara never got to know any of them. They were always surrounded by strangers.

New faces always looked in on them in the morning; strange voices woke them up; strange hands dressed them, combed their hair, put down their food before them, and took away their empty plates.

They were never sure if the next face or voice or hands would be friendly and gentle and tender, or rough and hard and dangerous.

In the beginning Klas and Klara studied each servant anxiously, but after a while they paid no attention to them. They got used to it. What difference did it make whether they were cheerful or grouchy? Next time, no matter what, there would be someone new.

One of the reasons the servants were changed so

often was that they broke so much glass. Recently, they'd been particularly slovenly and slipshod. Broken glass lay everywhere. New glass would be supplied immediately, but it would shatter just the same. And it proved to be impossible to find out who was to blame, for everyone denied everything, and they all protected each other.

A suspicious, unfriendly feeling grew in the House. Everyone spied on everyone else, but still no one managed to catch the guilty one. Everyone was baffled by how it could be done. Could someone be breaking the glass on purpose?

The Lord and Lady didn't bother themselves about it in the beginning. They bought new glass and said nothing about it. But when it got worse and worse and when the servants suspected one another, so that the House resounded with their quarrels, then something had to be done.

The Lord ordered his old and faithful servant, the coachman, to find out who was breaking the glass.

This coachman was ancient and deadly solemn. He was stony-faced, and never let on what he was thinking. His silent and swift way of moving around was terrifying, for he walked as if his boots never touched the floor, but skimmed along just above it. His steps were stiff and jerky. He walked through the rooms like a wound-up mechanical doll or a puppet led along by its strings. This gave him a very inhuman look.

Part Two

The coachman kept his plans and ideas to himself. He was sure he knew how to catch the guilty one.

First he got a large supply of glasses. These he planted in different places around the House so that he'd be able to tell right off which were breaking first and fastest. Then he would know what part of the House the criminal lived in.

The next step was to put more glass out again all over that part of the House and wait. Then he would creep around there like a dark spider circling its web. Doors opened and closed soundlessly, as if by themselves, when the coachman's grey, stiff face peered in and disappeared just as swiftly, and then popped up right afterward in the door to another room.

Staring after him, the servants shook their heads. "He's getting old," they said to each other.

And it was true, he was ancient, but not feeble. There weren't many young people who could speed by as swiftly as he. It was weird; he seemed to be everywhere at once.

So it was all the more puzzling that he didn't manage to trap the guilty one. Everything went on just the same. Glasses always crashed in places where he happened not to be. And several times he heard something break into a thousand pieces right in the next room, but when he opened the door there wasn't a trace or a clue. The room would always be empty, but he'd find a glass completely shattered on the floor.

And he never heard a footstep. It had to be someone who could walk as silently as he did. And someone who was just as sly and crafty, too.

It was baffling. It both frustrated him and egged him on to try even harder. Occasionally the Lord came to ask how it was going, if he had found any clues. But he said nothing; he was masterful at keeping quiet. And it didn't bother him that he had nothing to report.

Finally he thought up something really brilliant.

He had been wrong to put the glasses out in different rooms. This gave his enemy too many possibilities.

Of course he should have set them all out in the

same place. And never just one glass, but a great many.

And so he arranged a big table, as if for a party, full of glasses and crystal carafes. He placed high-branched candlesticks around the table and lit them so that the glasses glittered and sparkled really temptingly.

Then he left the room. He closed the door very carefully behind him so that no one could guess his plot. But he didn't walk away. He crept into a big empty closet in the next room. Slowly he pulled the door closed, leaving just a little crack open through which he could see who passed by. But he listened as hard as he could, too, because there was another door to the room where the glasses were and the guilty person just might use that one. And so there he stayed and waited and waited. But no one came. Not a sound was heard from the next room.

At last he grew very uncomfortable in the closet. He crept out and walked over to the door. He was very depressed. He opened the door soundlessly. Just then he heard a crash!

He stood still in the doorway. His face, as usual, expressed nothing, but his arms trembled impatiently, ready to grab their prize. He didn't believe his eyes. He held himself back for a moment because he didn't want to forget the smallest detail of the strange performance he saw before him.

The light in the room was soft and dim, for it was

winter and late in the day. Crouching shadows hovered in the corners. But on the table the high candles glowed cheerfully and lit up the only person there.

It was Klas.

He stood on one of the chairs at the table, holding a goblet in his hand. The glass glittered, and he stared into it with a weird expression on his face. He was at once sorrowful, defiant, and triumphant. Suddenly, with all his might, he smashed the glass down on the floor, he stepped over to the next chair and grabbed another glass.

Thus he circled the room until all the glasses lay in pieces on the floor. Then he crawled down to run away. He was barefoot. He ran silently and very fast.

But there stood the coachman, blocking his way.

He stood like a shadow among the other shadows in the room.

All he had to do was put out his arm to catch Klas. It all happened in silence, for the coachman was a master at keeping silent, and Klas was speechless.

There followed a great commotion. Who could believe it! The servants, who had been wrongly suspected, were outraged. Loudly, in offended tones of voice, they announced they would work no longer. The Lady came down with a headache and told the Lord once again that the children were his find and that he had to look after them himself.

The Lord said he was astonished. He repeated this several times. The children were so dutiful and well-behaved.

Naturally, Klas had to be punished, he said, and pondered the problem a long time. Then he talked to the coachman, who went off to get a stout stick.

It hurt the Lord, but Klas had to be whipped for what he had done so that he would never do it again. The Lord explained all this and then he let the coachman give Klas a whipping. But he wasn't to hit him very hard. . . .

Klas did it again. And then the coachman was ordered to hit him harder. And harder. And harder. But Klas still did it. Klara was ordered to spy on her brother. It didn't help. Klas could outwit anyone. He showed astonishing guile. He was as clever as a fox and as quick as a weasel.

What could have come over him? There must be something wrong. He couldn't bear to look at glass. And this even though his father had been a glassblower! It was all very baffling!

But perhaps the children had been by themselves too much? Could that be the trouble? The Lord decided to find them a governess.

And that was how Nana came into their lives.

10

THE FIRST TIME Klas and Klara saw Nana she was eating.

The Lady led them up to where Nana sat, spread out along a bench on one side of a table. It was evening, but no lamps had been lit, so the room lay in dimness.

Nana had stuffed one corner of a light-colored napkin into her neckband. At first all the children could see was the glow of her napkin.

Then they lifted their eyes and looked right into an enormous open mouth, where a white lump of pastry was being churned and mashed around. They stared bewitched until the mush was swallowed, the mouth closed and then shifted into a bright smile.

Nana said good evening to them, and then the Lady left them in her care.

At that moment the servants carried in another course. Nana gobbled it and the children in the same glance—a glance that said: to my taste or not?

The dish came up to her expectations, but she was doubtful about the children. Her small, dangerous eyes studied them and knew at once that they were unhappy.

It didn't matter what her opinion of them was—whether she liked them or not—she would devour them in any case. She was that sort.

There are no words to really describe Nana's size properly. In both body and spirit she was an enormous person.

The Lord had decided that a fat governess must surely be the best kind, and that's exactly why he had chosen Nana.

He told her that he didn't want any more trouble from the children. And indeed he didn't. He didn't need to think about them any more. He didn't even need to see them any more if he didn't want to, for they would live as if chained to Nana's body. She didn't let them out of her sight for an instant.

From then on Klas and Klara had no life of their own. They lived Nana's life. Just like the little, silent cockatoo, Nana's house pet.

This was a terrified little bird that hunched in its cage and listened very carefully to everything Nana said. It nodded anxiously whenever she turned to it to show that it was following what she said and agreed with her. It blinked its terrified little eyes fitfully; it twitched and twisted its poor little body.

No one knew whether the cockatoo had been born unable to speak or had lost its voice faced with the thundering torrent of Nana's words. The only sound it could get out now was a shrill screech that seemed to pierce the very marrow of everyone's bones. Fortunately, it didn't screech too often, only sometimes, in its sleep. No one could ever become hardened to that kind of noise. It would make the blood freeze in a person's veins. All the unhappiness in the world was pitched in that scream.

The cockatoo was called Mimi.

Klas and Klara were eager to get to know Mimi, but Nana wouldn't let them, and they were never able to. Mimi kept her eyes fixed on Nana. She never looked at the children. It was as if she didn't notice that they existed.

But soon it was the same with Klas and Klara, too.

They had to keep their eyes on Nana, or else things could go very badly for them.

Every other hour Nana had to have something to eat. Then a big table was arranged for her, and she sat down on one side, with the children opposite her. The table groaned under the plates and platters loaded with food. Nana never had any trouble thinking up tasty treats for herself. But the children only ate when they were ordered too, dutifully. Otherwise they sat staring down at the silver dinnerware or into Nana's enormous wide-open jaws.

Mimi perched in her cage next to Nana, who fed her the whole time with fig seeds that she kept in a bag. Mimi ate and swallowed them, dutifully and daintily, with the same seriousness a little schoolgirl shows, picking up knowledge from her teacher's hand. You could stuff any amount of seeds into her. It was miraculous, because Mimi wasn't a very big bird.

After she had eaten, Nana would yawn drowsily. She had to sleep to digest her food. Mimi seemed to pick up some strange kind of sleeping potion in Nana's glance, for she began to yawn immediately.

A big canopied bed had been brought into the children's room, and there Nana rested. As soon as she lay down, she fell asleep. It was as if a hurricane had swept through the room: first a murmur; then the roaring mounted, until at last she thundered. The curtains flapped like sails with her breathing, and the whole bed rocked like a ship in a stormy sea.

Mimi's cage, which hung from a hook under the canopy, swayed crazily, but Mimi would hide her head under a wing and sleep through it all as if nothing were out of the ordinary. And she never woke before Nana.

Klas and Klara had to lie down as well, of course, but they could never sleep. They lay there, scared out of their wits, abandoned, until the bad storm died down and Nana woke once more.

She never slept longer than fifteen minutes. Mimi awoke promptly at the same time.

On waking, Nana would be terribly sharp and dangerous.

This was when she would take charge of the children's education.

She owned a big trunk, in which she would root about and take out piles of books, abacuses, and slates to write on. Then she would begin her classes.

She tested Klas and Klara out of the books.

She hopped from one subject to another, from one book to another. And every time she closed a book, she slammed it so hard that the children shot up in the air. This she repeated again and again.

And they stood there like two foolish little idiots. They didn't know anything. They didn't learn anything. They understood nothing.

When it was obvious to her how dumb they were,

she would plan their education. She ran crazily around the room, her arms flapping about so that her little eyeglasses, far down on her enormous nose, bobbed and jumped wildly.

Streams of warnings and bullying and scolding flooded out of her mouth. Then she would stop suddenly right in the middle of the room and shout, "REPEAT WHAT I HAVE SAID!"

A disagreeable silence would follow. Klas and Klara were unable to say a word. Pressed back against the wall so that she wouldn't crush them, they stood there wild with terror. They looked as if they had been turned to stone. All their thoughts stood still.

Since they weren't able to answer her, Nana would come over and pinch them.

She had remarkably small, nimble hands and feet. In fact, her feet must have been very strong indeed to hold her up. And there was strength in her fingers, too. That Klas and Klara could vouch for.

Every time Nana beat them, she said she had never worked with such badly brought up children. They were impossible to educate—she couldn't make anything of them, she said, wheezing and puffing like a bellows. Yes, they were hopeless!

But then, even worse, the very worst, were her singing lessons. It was then they wished they were mute like Mimi. Nana was very demanding about singing.

Part Two

She would have been a singer, she told them, if only people didn't have something wrong with their hearing. And now she wanted to know if Klas and Klara had something wrong with their ears, too. So she would place herself right in the middle of the room and command them to listen carefully. She sang first, and then it was her idea that they should sing after her.

But she sang so high, so very high. And fright paralyzed Klas' and Klara's throats. They could only manage to squeak out tiny, hoarse peeps.

So Nana discovered that they, too, had something wrong with their ears. And ears like that had to be pinched. Never in all her life had she come across such unmusical ears, she said, and then she pinched them.

And this is how it went, day after day.

Klas and Klara sat at the table watching Nana eat. They lay in their beds listening to Nana sleep. They stood pressed against the wall facing the attack of Nana's teaching.

To be in Nana's care was to be in her clutches.

I I

THE LORD AND Lady were completely satisfied with
their governess. It was wonderful, too, how she was
teaching the children, though it wasn't necessary.
Her frequent singing lessons were perhaps a little
disturbing because Nana sang such high notes, but
she told them that the children were very unmusical
and had to practice often, so it really wasn't her
fault.

And there'd been no broken glasses at all since
Nana came to the House. No one could deny that
she was wonderful.

There was only one problem. You could overlook
the fact that she had to eat every other hour, but her
naps after eating were undeniably awkward. Not
because she slept, but because her sleep was so
noisy; she disturbed the whole House.

Every other hour, for fifteen minutes, all work
stopped throughout the House. Everyone looked at
everyone else in dismay: *Nana is sleeping again.*

It was more or less like a thunderstorm. There was

nothing anyone could do about it; the storm had to have its own way. No one was exactly scared, just shaken, riled, unable to get hold of himself until it had passed.

That's what it felt like when Nana slept.

The Lady suffered more than anyone else, for her bedroom was directly under the children's. The storms raged right over her head. She didn't feel that she ought to move just because of Nana. But finally, it was just too much.

She decided to move Nana instead. The children could be moved to another part of the House. But Nana would hear none of it. She said no, curtly. This room suited her. Here she kept her trunk full of school books, and here was her suitcase with all her costumes, which she always brought along in case she became an opera singer—and that's what she would have become if only people's hearing were a little better, she said, staring at the Lady's ears so accusingly that the Lady drew herself back. She had no desire to discuss ears with Nana.

Another time, when the Lord quietly tried to point out to Nana that both her suitcase and her trunk could be moved along with her, if necessary, he was pierced by such a fierce stare that he trembled.

"I WILL NOT be moved about!" thundered Nana, and there the subject was dropped. They would just have to find another solution.

One day the Lord came home with a huge bottle

of pills to cure snoring. Since the pills were supposed to quiet noises, he thought they might even help Nana. All he had to do was persuade her to take them. But she was easily riled, so he had to be careful not to upset her.

When she came in one morning complaining of exhaustion, the Lord hurried out and fetched the pill bottle. He told her the pills would give her a lot more energy, and that she should take one with every meal.

Nana took the pills and everyone waited excitedly.

But the only result was that she slept for half an hour instead of fifteen minutes. The terrible noises went on just the same.

Afterward she came and thanked the Lord and promised to go on taking the pills because she felt so much more energetic.

And so from then on the House was paralyzed for twice as long. It was a catastrophe.

The Lady had to take tablets to calm her nerves, and she wore ear plugs, too. She grew pale and looked rather frazzled. And there was nothing anyone could do about it, because everyone thought Nana's work was so important. Everything else in the House depended on her, or that's what people said, but in fact no one dared go against Nana. Everyone realized that Nana intended to stay there just as long as she pleased. Since her arrival, she was the one who gave the orders. And that was the whole truth.

The only ones who could take advantage of Nana's sleep were Klas and Klara. However strange it sounds, they had come to think of her naps as peaceful, restful times. A little freedom. For in spite of everything, Nana was less dangerous when she slept. And so half-hour naps were twice as good for them.

Mimi also slept through, and so, as soon as they both fell asleep, the children would creep out of their beds and leave the room silently. When Nana woke she would find them back in their beds again. They were very careful not to come back too late, because her naps were the only times they had to themselves.

In fact, there wasn't very much for them to do in the House, but they were free, and that was enough. At least in the beginning.

They walked as they used to up and down the stairs and played their old game: that the House was a mountain. But in some strange way the House had become more dangerous than before. Every day it seemed to grow bigger and darker, more frightening and grimmer. It was no good pretending that it was an ordinary old mountain on the ground. It had become a very threatening peak. It rumbled ceaselessly as if a giant lay there, ready to spring out, a sleeping giant who could wake up at any moment.

Klas said he wanted to play that they were going away from the mountain. He didn't want to just walk up and down. He wanted to get away some-

times. But Klara didn't know how to play that game. Perhaps that game didn't even exist. Perhaps there were mountains from which you could never escape.

They didn't know what to play any more.

They stood in the middle of the House on an endless double staircase with the growling roar rising and falling around them. All at once they realized how lonely they were. And they weren't just alone —people can want to be alone sometimes—they were abandoned, and that is much, much worse, because no one wants to be abandoned.

They slumped down on the steps.

Now, for the first time, they felt how vast the House was. They felt so comfortless, so lost, as if they were actually shrinking. The House was swallowing them up; they'd never find a way out; they would grow smaller and smaller. That's how it felt to them.

Then, through the rumble—from above, from below, from all sides—small, faint ticking sounds reached them. They listened excitedly. It was the clocks measuring time throughout the House. There were clocks in all the rooms, just as there were mirrors. And, from where the children sat, they could hear all the clocks ticking at once. It was as if all the ticking sounds were pitched to reach this one spot. And Klas and Klara listened excitedly: somehow there was comfort in the sound, a little hope.

The clocks could be heard despite the rumbling

roar. They hadn't stopped. They ticked along as if life depended on it.

Just then, asleep in her bed, Nana seemed to sense that the children were not listening to her, and that was inexcusable. She let out one great breath that silenced all the clocks in the House completely.

Like a wave high enough to cover the sky, the noise rose and engulfed all other sounds in the House. Nana was in command once again, she alone.

Klas and Klara stood up and took each other by the hand. They walked slowly up the stairs, sadder than ever before. Now all hope had gone. Even the clocks didn't exist any more. Nana had conquered time, too. For ever and ever into eternity, only she would be heard.

They turned down the corridor where they used to meet the Mirrorchildren, so long ago. That was before Nana had come. They had taken on themselves those children's sorrows because they had none of their own. But now they did have their own. They were the most unhappy children in the world. And they thought that perhaps the Mirrorchildren might be able to help them. Perhaps they had become happy again.

Yes, they just had to reach the Mirrorchildren.

They started running, but soon grew tired. The corridor was very long. They walked and walked. Why weren't the children coming to meet them? Why didn't they see any children there? They came all the way up to the mirror where they used to meet, where they used to stand, pressing their foreheads against those in the mirror, with only the glass between them.

But this time they didn't meet the Mirrorchildren. The mirrors were empty.

And then Klas and Klara understood that they had ceased to exist.

12

THE LORD WALKED from window to window, checking to see whether all his street lamps were alight. He did this every evening. They were always lit, but he checked them just the same.

From up there in the House they looked like small, pale lemon seeds arranged in rows. It was easy to see right away if any were out. But this had never happened—every evening the Lord was satisfied.

Otherwise he didn't have very much to be happy about.

The Lady was ill; she wouldn't leave her bed. The doctors claimed that she wasn't ill at all, yet she refused to get up.

Nothing amused her any more. Nothing.

The Lord paced back and forth through his rooms, deep in thought. He was a calm man, he never lost control, but now he thought this situation had gone on too long. It was just too much. He did everything, but never got any thanks. A very long time

had now passed since anyone had said thank you to him.

The Lord said to himself that he was definitely the only clever person in the whole world. He was the only one who realized what was wrong with the Lady. She couldn't wish, that was her whole sickness. It was crystal clear. But how could he get her to grasp that fact herself? Impossible. When he talked to her, she only sighed or hissed at him or burst into tears.

And she had never thanked him for the children. Properly speaking, he should have sent them back, since she was so ungrateful, but now they belonged to the House. He'd even got them a governess.

Nana, yes....

He wandered anxiously from window to window. Nana belonged to the House, too. It wouldn't do to argue with her. And that was something the Lady could understand. Nana was, actually, a most remarkable person, when she wasn't sleeping.

But that was it: if and when she wasn't sleeping, when she wasn't asleep. . . .

The Lord repeated this several times, wrinkling his forehead with thought.

For just at that moment Nana happened to be sleeping, and the thought got stuck in his mind. He went to the nearest window and counted the lemon seeds again. They threaded along for him, they seemed to hop, but he counted, anyway, to have something to do while Nana slept.

When she awoke, he returned to his thought.

The Lady had said something that he didn't know how to take. This was recently. He had, as usual, begged her to try to wish for something, so that everything would be all right again.

And then she had answered, "You might just as well beg me to do some magic."

What could she have meant by that? To wish and to perform magic were surely not at all the same. Next time he asked why she had said that, she only got angry with him. And then, though he asked her time and again, she never explained.

But yesterday she had answered suddenly, "My dear, I just mean that you'll need witchcraft to get me to wish for anything more in life."

Part Two

Witchcraft! What kind of witchcraft? He begged her to explain herself a little more clearly, but she only added, "I mean exactly what I say. Witchcraft."

It wasn't easy to understand.

Somehow, he had to find out what she meant. He paused at each window, pondering his problem. Truly he didn't have an easy time.

The mood in the House had grown even grimmer. This was for two reasons.

Nana's cockatoo, which couldn't sing, had begun to shriek in its sleep. And then glasses had started to shatter again. It was terrible.

Mimi might shriek as much as several times a day. The only person who didn't suffer from it was Nana, who was never even wakened by the sound. She insisted that Mimi only screamed because she was displeased with the children. She would scream whenever the children were stupid, said Nana. Klas and Klara were ashamed. It was a ghastly screech, awful, unwholesome, ill-boding, unbearable.

And glasses were shattering, too, while Nana slept. Not much, but it happened several times a day, regularly. And how it came about was a complete mystery, because this time the pieces didn't end up on the floor. Glasses lay shattered where they stood, yes, even inside a cupboard where the glasses were kept safely, they would be found broken in dainty, neat rows.

The whole thing was ghostly. The coachman took up his spying once again, but never caught anyone.

No matter how hard he worked, setting traps, he never caught anyone. He suspected Klas, but never was able to catch him redhanded.

He even began to doubt his own sanity. Glasses practically shattered right in front of his eyes without his catching a glimpse of Klas. It got to be too much for him, he felt so helpless and inefficient. He fell to brooding and complaining.

And so that winter passed, a black, desperate winter, without snow, without sun, without moon, and without stars.

The Lord wandered through the House counting his lamps; the coachman walked about spying and wringing his hands. And Klas and Klara tiptoed up and down the stairs and along the endless corridors searching for the Mirrorchildren. Mimi screeched. Glasses shattered. And all the while, Nana slept and the Lady wept.

13

IN THE VILLAGE where Albert and Sofia lived, life went on as usual.

Trees dropped their leaves and new ones unfurled, flowers faded and fresh ones bloomed, birds flew away and returned.

But Klas and Klara never came back.

Sofia wandered about the cottage brooding, and Albert stayed in his workshop. He just had to keep working. But the bowls he made always turned out like big, light-struck tears. Each one was different from the others, but also the same, for each in its own way reminded people of tears. No matter what he tried to make, they turned out that way, though he, himself, didn't notice it.

Nor could he understand why every single piece of his glassware sold at the fairs these days. He could never make enough. Albert was becoming famous. People came from near and far to buy from him.

He watched people clap their hands and sigh over

the beauty of his bowls. He watched with wonderment. People picked up the bowls so carefully, as if, at the very least, they were made of gold. He shook his head over it.

Though Albert didn't realize it, the people sensed something. They sensed that sorrow had made his bowls more beautiful. People have nothing against each other's tears—as long as they are beautiful to see.

But Albert got no pleasure from his success. Nor did he realize that he was becoming a very well-known glassblower. He didn't notice when people bowed to him; he was deaf to their compliments.

He could only think of his lost children.

He felt that he alone was responsible for their disappearance, for he alone had heard Flutter Mildweather's predictions. She had warned him that the children were going to disappear, and yet he had let it happen. At first when he heard her, he'd been terrified, and then later he hadn't believed it, because nothing had happened right away. How could he have been so foolish?

And now Flutter Mildweather had closed her doors to him. He might have been thin air as far as she was concerned. She had no more to say to Albert. Yes, he understood. In the village, she'd let it be known that she didn't intend to tell fortunes any more. It wasn't worthwhile for anyone to try asking her.

At home in the cottage Sofia blamed herself for everything. It was she who had brought misfortune on them all. It went back to that time when she had said that the children were only a bother. This was her punishment. She knew such words never went unpunished. Night and day she tormented herself with the thought; every waking moment it plagued her. And in her sleep the thought returned like a nightmare. Yes, she bore the blame: she was guilty, no one else.

And another thing pained her, too. She couldn't quite figure out what it was. But time and again a feeling came over her that she had forgotten something—something very important for her to remember.

Sometimes, in a flash, she'd feel that, if only she could remember what it was, everything would work out in the end.

What could she have forgotten?

She discussed it with Albert, but he only shook his head. She was brooding too much, he said, and that never did any good. Useless. And he was right, of course. It was just her imagination at work.

Nevertheless this feeling would sweep over her for an instant: yes, yes, that was it! The solution depended on her! She was certain that it was up to her. She must find it! The very next moment that certainty vanished again, and her despair seemed deeper than ever.

Albert would reason with her this way: if you've forgotten something, then you also know what it is you've forgotten. She was just the victim of her imagination.

One night Sofia woke with her heart pounding hard. She'd been sleeping soundly and dreaming of something, but she couldn't remember her dream.

Uneasiness drove her from her bed, her heart beating even more wildly, and, without really knowing what she was doing, she walked over to the little cradle that still hung from the ceiling in front of the open fireplace. A whole lot of odds and ends were stuffed away in the cradle. A length of flax hung down from it, shining like gold. She searched and searched, in a daze, without knowing what she wanted.

Suddenly she felt a little cold, hard object in her hand. She picked it up and carried it over to the window. She sat down where the moonlight flooded into the room. The object lay in the palm of her hand.

The ring Albert had given her long ago at the fair, the ring with the shifting green stone, lay in her hand. Oh dear, such a long time ago. . . .

She put it on her finger and studied her hands thoughtfully.

Suddenly, a great calm descended upon her. She sat there in the moonlight, remembering. It had been such a wonderful fair that season. Albert and she had been so happy, so very happy. . . .

Why had she stopped wearing the ring? That was stupid. The ring was very fine—she ought to wear it.

It was sweet of Albert to give it to her, though he really hadn't been able to afford it then. Absent-mindedly, she twisted the ring on her finger, sitting there deep in thought.

Suddenly her glance was drawn back to the ring.

Now she remembered why she'd put it away. It had upset and worried her.

Just as it did now. For again the very same forebodings returned: the stone seemed like an eye, and that eye watched her as she wore it.

She thought it blinked, and for a while she didn't dare move.

Then she held her hand out in the moonlight to look at it more clearly. She felt a chill and began shivering with fright. The stone had a look that terrified her. It was like a deep hole, a well, a ghastly sorrow, something inhuman.

After a moment it blinked again. It was repulsive.

Quickly she took off the ring and tossed it away from her by the window. She didn't dare look at it any more. Her heart beat wildly. What did this mean? Was she losing her mind?

Then her thoughts turned to the little old man who had sold them the ring, a really dreadful old man. Could he have bewitched it somehow? No, she really must calm herself. Here she was again, letting her imagination run away with her.

But there really had been something odd about that old man. Where had he disappeared to afterward? They'd never seen him before, or ever again.

And as for Flutter Mildweather, why, why had she behaved so strangely when she had caught a glimpse of the ring? What was it she had said?

Hadn't the old woman wanted the ring right away?

Sofia had gone to see her to have her fortune told, but Flutter hadn't wanted to . . . and then what?

Yes, what had happened then?

Now, once more, that feeling of certainty seized

Sofia, the certainty that she alone could solve their problem. She felt stronger than ever before. She felt surer, that the solution was here, right here, she had only to stretch out her hand. . . .

Where . . . where? Her memory still teased and taunted her, but she sat there quietly waiting . . . and, without knowing why, she reached out her hand and took up the ring. . . .

And then she remembered! Like a stroke of lightning she remembered what she had forgotten. Yes, now she knew.

She drew a deep breath. The moonlight quivered, trembled.

For one last time she let her eyes fall on the shifting green stone, deep into it. Far, far away she seemed to hear Flutter Mildweather's forgotten words, and her lips formed them silently.

"You're wearing a ring, Sofia. If misfortune should ever befall you one day, you must send me that ring, and I'll help you, wherever you may be. Don't forget my words! Send me the ring!"

Trembling a little with the memory, she kissed the ring.

After a while she rose, dressed, and walked out into the moonlight. The village lay there sleeping. But, up on the old Gallows Hill, a pale light shone from the window under the apple tree.

An owl shrieked.

The apple tree glowed with blossoms. A night

wind swept over the hill, and a few petals drifted down like snow.

The light up there flickered slightly.

The owl that had shrieked got no answer and shrieked again.

Sofia walked with her ring through the moonlight. She held the ring carefully in her hand, she didn't wear it, she wouldn't put it on. . . .

14

IT WAS NOW well past midnight.

Flutter Mildweather sat in her cottage, hunched over her loom, weaving. She stared thoughtfully at the pattern as if searching for something. The candle had almost burnt out in its holder. Taking it up, she held it high over her loom. The light flickered wildly.

Perched on the loom, Wise Wit the raven peered out the window. He watched the appleblossoms falling so gently and beautifully through the moonlight. He heard the owl screech.

With a sigh Flutter put down the candle. Wise Wit looked up at the moon and then she said to him, "Are you sitting there looking at the moon, Wise Wit?" she asked quietly.

"Yes," answered Wise Wit, "but I don't see it."

"No, you can only see the sun," said Flutter, patting her weaving reflectively. Then, after a pause, she asked, "You did fly over to All Wishes Town. Why can't I hear what is happening over there?"

Wise Wit sat just as before with his eye fixed on the moon. He didn't answer.

"I sent you there because I wanted to know what you saw," said Flutter Mildweather, moving the candle again uneasily, anxiously.

The raven hesitated and then answered that he hadn't seen anything except the children. Flutter stared at him, very disturbed.

"Nothing at all?" she asked.

No, Wise Wit hadn't seen a thing. He seemed upset by this, too, and so Flutter asked him no further questions. But she looked very troubled.

She knew what it meant when Wise Wit could see nothing with his one good eye: there hadn't been a single solitary good thing there at all, nothing beautiful to see, so he had seen nothing. A terrible thought came to her. What would he have seen if he'd had the other eye, too, the eye that saw only the evil in the world?

Terribly anxious, she grabbed a little roll of paper that lay on the floor. Wise Wit had brought it not long ago. It was a notice he had found tacked up on a tree by the road.

Flutter Mildweather had read it many times, and she read it now with growing displeasure. The ornamented letters spelt out:

WOMAN SKILLED IN WITCHCRAFT

preferably elderly, solomonic,
experienced in astrology and other magical arts
sought immediately.
Private room with telescope.

The Lord

Why had Wise Wit bothered to drag this all the way home? There were always a great many different notices on trees along the roads. He usually didn't bother with them at all.

What did this one have to do with her?

She'd sent the raven to All Wishes Town as a scout, but he had returned with nothing to relate. Was he hiding something from her? He seemed remarkably secretive these days.

In any case, she had no intention of traveling there. Her whole being rose up in protest against the idea. And so she threw away the roll of paper with uncharacteristic fierceness and temper.

"Solomonic!" she sniffed to herself. "What in heavens does that mean?"

"Like King Solomon, of course," Wise Wit explained immediately.

"Yes, yes," said Flutter impatiently, "but I'm not going, anyway. Not now when you won't tell me what's happening there."

But the raven answered quietly, "Better seen than heard."

"That's what you say. . . ."

"The wise have long ears and short tongues," said the raven, and shoved his head under his wing as a sign that, as far as he was concerned, their conversation was over. But Flutter shook her head. Obviously Wise Wit wanted her to go to All Wishes Town for some reason, and she didn't intend to.

She sighed and looked down again at her weaving. She wasn't enjoying this carpet, for the pattern was confusing her. She was finding it more and more difficult every day. It upset her; she could hardly bear it any longer. This was the most difficult pattern she had ever woven on her loom.

Wise Wit looked as if he wanted to go to sleep. And Flutter Mildweather plunged deeper into her thoughts. The candle flickered. Time passed.

Then the owl shrieked again.

Wise Wit turned, and Flutter Mildweather looked up from her loom. They glanced at each other and listened. It was very quiet. . . .

Then all of a sudden someone knocked on the door . . . several times.

The two of them waited anxiously where they were. Then the knocking began again, and went on without stopping. The raven didn't move, but Flutter rose slowly and walked over to open the door. She walked with weary steps, while the desperate knocking continued as if life depended on it. Filled with strange forebodings, she hesitated before unbolting the door. A desperate conflict raged within her, for she sensed that dark powers were on the move that night, and she was not yet certain that she had them in her control.

Loudly the knocking insisted. And then she opened the door.

When the door swung wide, the moonlight streamed in. Outside stood Sofia, the glassblower's wife. She was very pale and breathing heavily.

They studied each other in the dazzling moonlight. Wordlessly, they looked deep into each other's faces.

Then Sofia quickly stretched out her hand.

"Here," she gasped for breath. "Here is the ring. . . ."

Without answering, Flutter Mildweather took the ring, looked at it, and slipped it quickly into her skirt pocket.

Their eyes met again. Sofia's were round, dark, desperately pleading. Flutter's were neither flowerlike nor their usual mint blue.

Perhaps it was only the moonlight that made her glance so intense, so burningly strong and dangerous as it was now. Something about her in that instant was not like her old self. Her whole form seemed to grow larger and shimmer with mystery, a mystic apparition. Sofia felt this and was afraid but also confident. She thought of reminding Flutter about her promise, but the words died on her lips, for she knew there was no need to.

She only nodded and turned and ran down the hill, filled with an inexplicable joy. There was hope. . . . Miracles could happen. . . . Now and always.

Flutter Mildweather left the door wide open and walked back into the room with the moonlight flowing like a train behind her.

The candle had by now almost burnt out, and Wise Wit rested with his head tucked under his wing. Flutter stood for a while watching him.

Then she walked over to the loom and with one finger traced a dark thread running through the pattern. She was calm once again; her lips moved and shaped words full of mystery and beauty. Nothing in the weaving looked confused or disconnected any longer. Everything was clear and wonderfully easy to understand.

She followed thread after thread with her finger, a secret, powerful strength growing within her, overcoming all her doubts. She drew herself up, looked again at Wise Wit—he had been right—she took up the little roll of paper and tossed it into the fire, where it instantly burst into flames.

"So now let us set off, Wise Wit," she said to the sleeping raven. She lifted him up and returned him to his cage. He slept on undisturbed.

She put on her cloak with the shoulder cape. She was already wearing her hat. Ridiculous as it may seem, a little bundle containing two glass bowls wrapped in rags and the bird cage were all she needed on her journey.

One last glance around the room. She stood there pondering until the candle snuffed out in its holder and the flames died to embers in the fireplace.

Then she left the cottage, locked the door, and stepped out onto the hill with the sleeping Wise Wit in his cage. She smiled. . . .

And then, immediately, they disappeared in a cloud of apple blossoms and moonbeams.

15

WHEN THE LORD was informed that Flutter Mild-weather had arrived at the House, he went down to greet her himself.

"Welcome, my good lady," he said very graciously, though a little ashamed that he should need the help of someone like Flutter Mildweather. He thought about this while he acted the good host. He tried to turn the whole situation into a joke.

"Since we have neither a church nor a theatre here in town, we might as well enjoy a little witchcraft these days," he said, laughing his dry little laugh.

Flutter stared at him—mint blue—but didn't answer. For the first time in his whole life, the Lord felt unsure of himself. This remarkable woman had more to tell him than he thought.

"Well, I hear these are hard times for witches and magicians," he said nervously. "A wizard of the old school can lose his audience. . . ."

He stopped speaking. The awesome old lady stared at him, her eyes turning bluer and bluer.

"Now personally, I have nothing against witches,"
he added patronizingly, "Not at all, but. . . ."

He paced back and forth to show that he was
thinking. The old lady stood there smiling. What
was there to smile about now? He really must say

something to make her understand that he wasn't terribly impressed by her witchcraft.

"This whole thing is completely the Lady's idea," he said, "because actually I would have preferred a dwarf or a little fool, though I gather these are hard times for fools, too. . . ."

"Not that I've noticed, dear sir," said Flutter Mildweather.

Those were the first words she had uttered, and the Lord immediately fell silent.

He who had never cared much about any one single person and therefore could boast that he loved "all mankind," now felt that this old lady thought rather badly of him. He wanted to tell her to go, but for the Lady's sake he had to persuade her to stay.

He showed her the way up to the tower where her room was prepared, and it actually did contain a telescope. With a sweeping gesture he explained that, if she needed anything else, she need only ask. As he prepared to leave, Flutter Mildweather called out to him.

"I'd like to know what is expected of me," she said.

The Lord raised his eyebrows.

"Didn't I tell you? Well, your task is to get the Lady to wish."

"Wish? And what should she wish for?"

"Whatever she wants. She says, she insists that witchcraft is required to get her to wish for anything ever again. Well, of course, that is nonsense. Nevertheless, Madam, that is why you are here."

He paced impatiently back and forth as he talked. It was obvious that he thought Flutter Mildweather ought to be able to know all this without being told.

"Where can I meet the Lady?" asked Flutter.

"In her room, of course." And the Lord explained where her room was. Then he said goodbye abruptly. At the door he turned and said, with an exhausted expression, "Remember now, Madam, your task is only to make the Lady wish again. It doesn't matter what she wishes for. Then naturally I, personally, will fulfill her wishes. Is that absolutely clear?"

"Absolutely," answered Flutter Mildweather with such a peculiar smile that the Lord hastily closed the door.

Flutter put down the birdcage in which Wise Wit had been sitting all the while, silently but attentively. Now she let the raven out and asked him what he thought of the Lord.

Wise Wit flew up and perched on the telescope before he answered. Then he said vaguely,

"Not everyone is equally wise. A small sea has a short coast line, isn't that so?"

"Yes," replied Flutter. "Yes, indeed."

Then she asked the raven to scout around the House, while she set off to visit the Lady.

Part Two

"Oh yes," yawned the Lady, as Flutter Mild-weather entered her room. Then she turned away indifferently and went on talking, "You must be Mademoiselle Mildweather. Please sit down."

She lay in her bed surrounded by soft pillows. She pointed to a chair with a tired gesture. Flutter sat down silently and the Lady continued wearily,

"I understand that Mademoiselle has come here to entertain me with her magic arts. Fine. Do what you like, but don't bewitch me! That I won't endure."

She shut her eyes.

"Life isn't so simple that you can unravel it with a little hocus pocus. But surely Mademoiselle must realize that better than anyone else. . . ."

She fell silent, and neither of them spoke for a

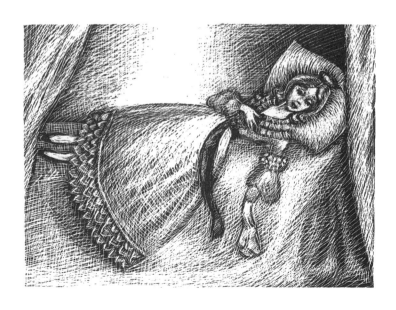

while. Flutter watched intently while the Lady lay there, so beautiful, so weary. She kept her eyes closed; she hadn't even glanced at Flutter yet. She merely lay there motionless. Now she started talking again.

"Mademoiselle isn't very talkative. Mademoiselle hasn't said anything yet."

"I only talk with people who look at me," answered Flutter quietly.

The Lady made a weak gesture with her hand but didn't look up.

"Well, that's fine," she said, her voice trailing off. "Then you'll have to listen to me, and I won't have to see or hear you. Isn't that a little disappointing for someone who is a witch?"

"Quite the contrary," replied Flutter Mildweather. "That's just as it should be."

Then the Lady opened her mouth wide and yawned.

"Oh, well then," she said, disappointed, "what can I think of to insult you? Oh yes, I know you and the Lord are plotting to get me to start wishing again, but that's a waste of time and energy. . . . Are you such a fool, Mademoiselle, as to waste your time? You'll be sorry if you think I'm that stupid. No, don't count on me being a fool. Save your ridiculous little acts for someone else. Someone more stupid. . . ."

She paused a moment and yawned, then continued spinning on the same thread:

"I'm just vain and idle, not stupid. Now my Lord

is both vain and stupid and so he's a happy person,
as you, Mademoiselle, must have seen. . . . And he
can afford to be nice, too, whereas I can't. I'm
wicked . . . very wicked. . . ."

Flutter Mildweather still said nothing, but she listened carefully all the while. They were really
chatty here in the House, both the Lord and his
Lady.

Now the Lady raised her voice.

"I am WICKED," she repeated. "DON'T YOU
HEAR ME, Mademoiselle? Why don't you
disagree?"

Flutter was silent as a stone wall.

Then the Lady looked up for the first time.

"I AM USED to people contradicting me when I
say something bad about myself," she said with wide
open eyes.

"Is that so?" commented Flutter. "And I'm used
to agreeing."

The Lady sat up in her bed and stared Flutter up
and down, down and up. She looked childishly displeased, but then her old indifference won out. And
her haughty pride.

Her scornful glance fell on Flutter Mildweather's
left ring finger.

"What is that ring you have there?"

"It's just an old silver ring."

"Yes, I can see that, but it doesn't even have a
stone in it. Did you lose it?"

"Yes, it is gone . . . now."

The Lady shivered.

"Ugh, it looks unsightly," she said. "Just as if it were blind. Take it off immediately."

But Flutter Mildweather shook her head and the ring stayed right where it was.

The Lady sighed and fell back against her pillows.

Then, like a shadow, a servant suddenly glided noiselessly across the room. He placed a tray with a glass of water and several tablets on the bedside table. Then he disappeared again.

Immediately afterward, a frightening wheezing noise started to build in the air. It sounded as if a hurricane were sweeping through the House, for everything trembled and shook.

The Lady pressed both hands against her face for a moment. Then she took out a pair of ear plugs, put them in her ears, and, with trembling hands, shoved the tablets into her mouth and swallowed them down with water. She looked blankly at Flutter and said in an irritated voice,

"You may go now, Mademoiselle. You've sat here far too long already. Why are you still here? I have no desire to talk to deaf ears. And I don't want to talk when I don't know what I'm saying, and how can I know what I'm saying when I can't hear my own voice? You should have realized that by now. —GO AWAY!"

Flutter Mildweather got up and hastily left the room.

16

MEANWHILE, NANA HAD discovered that Klas and Klara crept off during her naps. It so happened that one time she forgot to take her pills and woke after only fifteen minutes' sleep. The children's beds were empty, and she found them out on the stairs. Naturally there was a terrible commotion. Everyone was sure they had found an explanation for why glasses broke while Nana slept. She, herself, was convinced of it.

She immediately asked the Lord for a big bracelet and two smaller ones. There was a hook on each of the smaller bracelets and two on the big one. She also asked for two long chains. From then on, Klas and Klara had to wear the bracelets all the time, and Nana wore the big one. Every time she lay down, she hooked the chains to her bracelet and attached one to Klas and the other to Klara. So then the children had to lie dead still in their beds, for

Nana would feel their slightest movement and wake. Despite her loud snoring, she never slept very deeply.

But when Nana turned over in her canopy bed, she pulled the children's chains toward her and sometimes she twisted about so violently that their arms were jerked out from under their covers. Sometimes their whole beds were pulled toward her, too.

Nana felt she was being very crafty and clever. She was sure all the glass breakage was over now for good. But she was mistaken.

Despite the fact that both children were chained to her and couldn't possibly leave their beds, glass broke somewhere in the House almost every time she went to sleep.

No one was able to figure out how it happened.

Flutter Mildweather learned of this mystery on the first day she came to the House.

She had just left the Lady's room when Mimi screamed in her sleep. Flutter was not easily terrified, but this scream was so ghastly, so heart-shattering, that she stopped, unable to move.

When she had calmed herself, she walked quickly in the direction of the scream. The deafening thunder that filled the House came from the same place.

Flutter's heart beat hard and fast, and she was filled with awful forebodings.

She saw nary a soul the whole time. Room after room stood empty, but everywhere she found glass shattered on the furniture. It looked most curious and strange.

On one table a vase lay in smithereens. The flowers had scattered, and the water dripped down onto the floor.

In another place, an empty bowl had burst. On a side table a serving tray held broken wine carafes. The different wines dripped silently onto the carpet, staining it slowly redder and redder. And there was not a person in sight.

She walked faster and faster, until she was bounding along, hunting through the rooms. An unusual, overpowering alarm filled her, for she felt sure she would soon face the awful secret.

Who was breaking the glasses? Who was screaming?

Where were the children?

The awful uproar continued. She slowed down. She realized she was very near to it now. Then Wise Wit came flying to meet her on his silent wings. Without a word he settled on her shoulder. This calmed her.

They met in front of a big window overlooking the whole town. It was springtime, about three in the afternoon. It should have been light outside, but an eternal grey rain drilled down on the road ruts and darkened the day.

"Did you find out anything, Wise Wit?" asked Flutter.

The raven nodded and looked toward the door to the next room.

"Are the children in there? Have you been in there?"

He nodded again and stayed on Flutter's shoulder while she walked up to the half-open door. She opened it and paused for a moment in front of the thick, dark green curtain. Then she drew it aside with a firm hand and walked into the room.

The windows were closed. A green darkness filled the room. When she had accustomed herself to the darkness she noticed an enormous canopy bed by one wall, and, opposite it against the other wall, two children's beds.

Chains ran across the room from the canopy bed to each child's bed. They shone in the sickly light and rattled every time whoever lay in the canopy bed breathed.

Trembling, but not hesitating, Flutter walked right over to the big bed. The sound of her steps was lost in the storm around the sleeping figure.

Flutter turned pale, and even her eyes seemed to lose their color. They shone with a strangely distant light. The raven perched motionless on her shoulder.

High up in the canopy bed swung a cage in which a bird slept. Wise Wit looked up at it sharply while Flutter kept her eyes fixed on the person in the bed. First she thought a pair of eyes were beaming out at her from the dark, and then she saw it was only a pair of glasses.

At the same instant she recognized the person in the bed. She shut her eyes with an expression of the deepest pain and suffering.

She rubbed her forehead as if to brush away the sight, but then she looked up, leaned over the sleeping figure, and whispered sorrowfully, "I suspected as much. It really couldn't have been anyone else but Nana. What have you been up to now, my poor sister?"

It was a terribly difficult moment for Flutter, who hadn't seen her sister in a very long time and certainly would have wished their meeting to be different. This explained the despairing gentleness in her voice.

But now Nana turned restlessly in her sleep, the chains rattled, and Wise Wit flew up with a cry of warning and disappeared into the folds of the drapery.

Flutter gave Nana just one more glance full of compassion and agony before she slipped out of the room.

In the next instant, Nana and Mimi woke up and the House fell silent again. But it was a silence that seemed spooky to Flutter as she wandered back the way she had just come, with Wise Wit flying before her.

When she passed by a large ballroom, she saw an old coachman holding a broken bowl in his hands. His face had an extraordinarily stiff expression. He didn't notice her.

In another room she saw him again. This time he was holding the shattered pieces of a vase. He didn't see her there, either.

A third time she caught sight of him with a broken wine carafe. He had wine on his hands, and he didn't look up.

She marveled how he could move so swiftly and still give the impression that he always stood fixed in the same spot. But then she forgot about him.

For she had other things on her mind.

Up in her tower room, she fell to pondering. The tower had windows on all sides, but the rain streamed down relentlessly until evening, when it stopped. The clouds dispersed and night brought back the stars.

Then Flutter went over to the telescope and aimed it at the heavens.

She wasn't surprised to find the same kind of loops and patterns up there that she saw in her weaving at home, only these were much bigger and more beautiful.

Many clever people maintain that you can find a connection between people and the stars. She didn't think that. She sniffed at the thought. That would be presumptuous. A likeness was what she could see, but not a connection.

No, everything in its place. And down here on earth people were her concern.

Up there the planets moved eternally. It comforted her to think that, however things might work out on earth, the stars would always be the same.

Wise Wit thought so, too.

"Every man lives his own life," said he, "no matter what befalls the stars."

17

A COUPLE OF days passed.

Color returned to the Lady's fair cheeks, and she rose from her bed. Then she sent for Flutter Mildweather and argued with her tirelessly. This arguing seemed to agree with her.

Now she was standing by an open window in her room. A gentle breeze played through her beautiful hair. The sun shone.

"Mademoiselle, what did you just call me? You know you must call me 'my Lady,'" she said irritably.

Flutter Mildweather stood beside her. She was wearing her cloak, for she had been on her way out when the Lady had sent for her. She answered now, "Oh no, she who is not mistress of herself is not a Lady." She spoke calmly and simply, without a trace of scolding.

It was such a beautiful day, the first fine day after

so many dark and grey ones. Even up here in the north, finally even in All Wishes Town, summer had come. The mild weather could be felt especially here in the grim and dreary House.

Flutter lifted her face to the sky. She smiled and slipped far away in her thoughts.

"You have no manners at all," she heard the Lady say. "When I want you to oppose me, you agree, and when I want approval, you disagree."

"I only say what I think," answered Flutter Mild-weather quietly and calmly, busy with her own thoughts. She felt bright and confident, ready for her task. She felt sure she could handle it today. It was a good day to travel.

"You mustn't say what you think. You should say what you know others are thinking. Don't you know that?"

"No."

"Then I'll have to teach you, Mademoiselle."

"It's not worth it."

"Anyway, it's not worth your trying to get me to wish anything," sighed the Lady wearily.

Flutter searched for her voice as if from afar, for she had been miles away in her thoughts.

"No, I don't think I'll bother about that either. There are much more important things in life. . . ."

With a violent, angry movement, the Lady shouted, "How can you say that! What is? WHAT is more important?"

Flutter went on looking up at the sky. She didn't answer straight away. A mist, a soft perfume of summer blossoms, of jasmine, reached her. . . .

Then she said, "Oh, so very much. Most everything is more important than a person's wishes. What do they matter?"

The Lady was silent. She looked astonished but not angry. She didn't know what to make of it. She didn't understand this horribly dressed old lady . . . nor did she understand herself. She felt at the same time both weak and furious, sorrowful and aroused.

Life had been much simpler before. For several years now she had experienced only grief and mortification. These new emotions were so unfamiliar that she scarcely knew what to do about them or how to handle them. It was all the old woman's fault. She wanted to hurt Flutter, to insult and sneer at her. But she couldn't. Everything she said fell flat on the floor.

And now this old lady announced that her wishes weren't important. That was inexcusable, not to be lightly dismissed or forgiven. But why didn't it anger her?

Why did this great insult only make her feel very relieved? Here she was, unable to talk back.

She followed Flutter's glance and said, indifferently, "I see you're gaping up at the clouds. What are you staring at?"

"The clouds. They look like little white lambs

wandering through the pastures of Paradise up there between the turrets."

Suddenly the Lady looked like a little girl. She said nothing. The birds' songs rose outside the window. She tilted her head gently to one side and looked up at the clouds.

Her voice had changed completely when she finally spoke. "Did you know that I was a shepherdess when I was a little girl? It was in a poor little pasture, not exactly a heavenly meadow, but beautiful, nevertheless. That was long, long ago. . . ."

The breeze lifted her hair and blew curls across her eyes. She brushed them aside and went on talking through the birdsong in the same serious voice. "Then I always longed to be rich and have everything I wanted. I never thought it would happen. It did. I got everything and then some. That's why I have stopped wishing, you see. It isn't only because I am wicked. . . ."

Then Flutter looked at the Lady. Their eyes met for the first time, and both realized that deep inside they were friends. Flutter was overjoyed, but the Lady was caught off guard and grew frightened. In her confusion she tried to look scornful when Flutter Mildweather said, "One almost always gets what one wishes—one just doesn't know when or how—and that's what makes wishing so frightening. One must wish for what one is able to accept, somehow or other. That's very important to bear in mind. . . ."

The Lady left the window and walked to and fro impatiently.

"Anyway, I decided not to wish at all," she said vehemently. "Why can no one understand that you can wish to keep your wishes just as they are? Here in the House, I never get to keep a single wish because they are fulfilled even before I've been able to feel I'm wishing, and that's awfully cruel. . . ."

She came back to the window and took Flutter's arm. Her eyes glistened.

"I turned wicked because of that. I want to be, I have to be wicked, especially to the Lord, because he's the one who steals them. He steals them because he has no wishes of his own, so he doesn't know what he's missing."

She dropped Flutter's arm and looked desperately around for help.

"I like the Lord, Mademoiselle, and so I'll be wicked to him until he understands. Yes, indeed I will."

A servant slipped into the room like a shadow and put down a tray with tablets, a glass of water and the ear plugs, then rushed out again.

The Lady followed him with her eyes. She looked frightened and sighed.

"Nana is about to fall asleep again. Come with me for a drive, Mademoiselle. It's so beautiful outside. I'll ask the Lord to come along."

She rang and ordered her coach. Her eyes took on the desperate, hunted expression they always had whenever Nana slept.

"Be quick about it now!" she shouted after the servant and then turned to Flutter. "I cannot harden myself to endure Nana's sleep," she said. "It drives me to despair."

And then Flutter took the occasion to ask, quietly, "Why don't you tell Nana to leave?"

The Lady looked bewildered and nervously guilty. She explained that Nana belonged to the House, and the children had to have a governess.

"Let the children go back to their parents," said

Flutter, emphasizing each word carefully, her eyes a very piercing blue.

"That's easy enough to say," replied the Lady impatiently. "They were actually the Lord's discovery, and now they belong to the House, too. . , ."

"Ahah," said Flutter. "So that's it? And perhaps I belong to the House, too?"

"Of course you do; that's obvious. Come along now, let's be off."

But Flutter Mildweather stood her ground. And the Lady, against her will, was held by the blue, blue eyes.

"When the time comes, I'll show you who belongs to the House and who doesn't," said Flutter, as clear as moonlight.

In that moment, Nana's sleep began, and the Lady fled from the House with Flutter following after her.

The Lord was already waiting in the coach.

They set off at great speed.

18

THE LORD HAD decided that he was going to be polite to Flutter Mildweather. The old lady obviously had some merit, for his Lady looked so much more cheerful now. And that was the main thing.

Noble and generous as he was, he didn't intend to reveal that he could hardly stand the old woman.

They drove slowly down the streets and the Lord proudly showed off his town. He pointed out where the big square would be, where the church would stand, the town hall, the theatre, the public baths, the school.

He described each building in the smallest detail: he lost himself in pillars and columns, in vaults and curving bays. He rambled on about the parks in the town, what magnificent kinds of trees and flowers he would set on display there.

It was to be the world's most beautiful and best town, he explained, and Flutter Mildweather understood right away that that was the very reason it would never be.

Meanwhile the Lady hunched down against the cushions in the coach and said nothing. She kept her eyes closed all the time until they had passed through the town's gates and left it behind them.

She looked up for the first time when they came out into the countryside.

Round about them summer flourished. It had arrived suddenly, completely. At the same time it seemed overwhelming. Throughout the long winter, she always managed to forget how marvelous it was.

She saw once more the cloud lambs nibbling in the blissful, enclosed meadows, as Flutter had said. She tried to catch Flutter's eyes and felt again that they were friends, and this no longer frightened her. She really didn't understand how it had come about, how the two of them could be friends, but she didn't mull over it any longer.

For a while she remained silent, and forgot everything around her. She breathed in the soft air and listened only to the birdsong.

She forgot All Wishes Town and the House and everything that had come to pass. She remembered only what it had been like when she was little and poor and barefoot, running through the grass gathering flowers. She tried to remember what flowers she used to pick, which ones she liked best, and suddenly she smiled and said in a soft, dreamy voice, right out of the blue, "I wish I had a bouquet of wild roses. But only the buds. When I was little, I always used to pick them before they came out. . . ."

The Lord, who had been sitting deep in his own broodings, turned and looked swiftly at Flutter Mildweather. His face lit up as if she had worked a miracle. Then he leaned forward to the Lady and announced ceremoniously,

"My dear . . . you have expressed a wish."

Terrified, the Lady opened her eyes wide, and then slowly closed them again. She didn't answer, but her lips trembled in surrender.

And then the Lord said with a proud and victorious smile, "Just as soon as we come to a wild rose bush, I'll fulfill your wish, my dear."

It was silent in the coach. Only birdsong could be heard. The horses galloped through the landscape, which grew more and more beautiful. They followed alongside a wandering stream, past meadows full of flowers and blooming hedges by the ditches. Everywhere blossoms nodded and swayed in the grass, but there were no wild roses to be seen.

A strange, intense excitement seized the three people in the coach. The Lord peered out anxiously but smiling all the while. The Lady kept her eyes tight shut, her face expressionless. And Flutter Mildweather sat bolt upright staring into the distance with her mint blue eyes.

No one dared say anything.

They seemed to be in a dream; the horses' hoof-beats, the birdsong, and the cloudlike perfume of the blossoms separated them from reality.

When they came to the fringe of the woods where the wild rose bushes grew, the Lord bade the coachman stop. He stepped out and walked across the fields toward the woods.

The Lady didn't watch him; she sat just as she had before, as did Flutter. They said nothing to each other while he was away, though nothing prevented them from speaking.

A long while passed before the Lord returned. He was empty-handed. He walked slowly, hanging his head low.

Finally the Lady looked up. Her face was excited and very serious.

"Where is my bouquet?" she demanded.

"All the roses are already fully in bloom," he answered dejectedly. "There wasn't a single bud."

"Don't I get my bouquet?" she asked, surprised.

"No," answered the Lord in great agony.

"Not at all?"

He looked completely crushed. He promised to send everyone out looking for wild rose buds, if only she would be patient.

But the Lady answered, "No, I want them now! From you!"

Then he begged her to wish for a bouquet of full-

blooming wild roses instead, but she shook her head solemnly.

"Why should I wish that?" she said. "That I can have."

Overwhelmed and contrite, he stood there on the road, but then she did something unexpected. She stretched out both her hands to him and smiled.

"Thank you, my friend," she said gently. "Thank you for finally letting me keep my wish."

He gazed at her in bewilderment, but happily, too; happy to hear her say the words he loved, "thank you."

And then she smiled at him again and said, "Now you have given me something that no one can take away from me. If you had given me the wild rose buds I had wished for, then they would have come out fully before the evening and in the morning they would have dropped their petals. Now they will always stay closed, tiny rose buds that will never open and never drop their petals, just as I wished. Thank you for letting me keep them!"

The Lord climbed back up into the coach and looked at Flutter Mildweather. He didn't know what to think, but she was smiling, too. He felt uncertain. It seemed as if he had done something good without knowing it.

A foolish thought came to him. Perhaps he could only do good things here in life. But then he instantly chased the thought away. Strangely enough, it didn't interest him. Right now such thoughts neither tempted him nor held him in their power. He heard only the Lady's voice.

"Now do you understand?" she asked faintly.

And he heard himself reply, "No, not yet—but I think I will understand."

19

NANA DIDN'T KNOW that Flutter Mildweather was in the House. Nor did Klas and Klara, though they wouldn't have remembered her.

Flutter had decided not to let herself be seen by them until the contest between herself and Nana had begun. Instead, she sent Wise Wit off to keep an eye on everything that went on between Nana and the children.

The raven flew like a soundless shadow high up under the eaves. The only one who saw him was Mimi, who was both mute and silent as a tomb. And even if Mimi had been able to speak, she wouldn't have said anything to Nana, because she didn't mind another bird coming into the House, and she and Wise Wit had exchanged secret looks of understanding.

In this way Flutter Mildweather got to know all of Nana's habits—how she gave lessons to the children and how she carried on in general.

She decided, finally, to attack during a singing lesson, for then Nana was always in her element. Then she was thoroughly refreshed and dangerous, for singing, which was her hobby, gave her strength.

It may seem odd that Flutter didn't choose one of Nana's weak moments instead, but that would have been unthinkable. Flutter wanted them to be equally matched. There would be no real test of strength if one of them set a trap for the other. Nana couldn't be given the opportunity to choose the moment of their struggle herself. It wouldn't do, however much Flutter would have liked to, because Nana had absolutely no scruples about fair play. She was completely without conscience; underhanded, wily, malicious, and full of deceit.

But they were sisters, nevertheless. Nana, like Flutter, was a force of nature; neither of them could be called ordinary or simple, and they both knew that. The fight between them had to be according to the laws of the wild: the stronger would win. For good or for evil.

Therefore, it wouldn't be right to attack Nana in one of her weak moments. If you really want to conquer evil, you have to face all its power and potential: you can't use trickery. And this was the case with Nana.

Flutter knew that, and her preparations did not include only her sister.

First and foremost, she invited the Lord and the

Lady to come to Nana's singing lesson with the children that day.

They didn't want to at all—what did the lessons have to do with them? But when Flutter insisted, the Lady quickly agreed and then the Lord, too. They remembered their happy drive through the countryside and promised to go. For, in some dim way, they realized that the old lady had had something to do with it, though it seemed that she had just sat there in the coach without doing anything.

Then Flutter rushed up to her tower chamber and exchanged a few words with Wise Wit. They agreed about something. After that, Flutter settled down for a little calm contemplation. She opened all the windows around the tower, and sat there a while, surrounded by the murmuring breezes of the summer. And thus she prepared to meet Nana.

When the singing lesson began, Flutter Mildweather made her way down to the room where Nana was with the children. Over her head, Wise Wit swept through the air on his strong wings. Flutter carried two of Albert the glassblower's bowls. When she met the Lord and the Lady she gave them each a bowl and asked that they hold them throughout the lesson. They were not to put them down.

The Lady looked at the bowls in fear and awe.

"Why, they look like tears!" she exclaimed.

"They are tears," answered Flutter Mildweather grimly.

They stared at her wonderingly. They didn't understand what she was getting at, but all they dared do was follow as she walked briskly into the room where Nana was.

The lesson had already begun.

Neither Nana nor the children noticed the three of them enter the room. Flutter signaled to the Lord and Lady that they should stand still and keep quiet.

Green light seeped into the room. The windows were covered with thick, tangled creeping vines. The curtains, like the walls, were green.

Nana stood in the center of the room, singing.

Klas and Klara huddled back against the wall staring at her as if they had been turned to stone. Mimi sat in her cage near the ceiling.

When Nana stopped singing, there was an anguished, trembling instant, while she glared at the children with her bulging eyes.

After the silence had had its full effect, she spoke, raising her piercing voice higher with each word,

"Now we'll hear whether there's anything wrong with your ears, children! Sing! SING! SING!"

Out of Klas and Klara came their usual hoarse, terrified, breathless peeps.

Then Nana started shaking with rage. She pressed her hands together and walked toward the children with slow, menacing steps.

But something happened that she hadn't expected. Klas and Klara caught sight of Wise Wit, who urged them to run.

Nana didn't see Wise Wit, but she flew into a terrible wild rage. With two awful strides, she caught up with the children, swept them up in her powerful arms, and grabbed hold of their ears.

"Did you think two such unmusical pairs of ears could get away without being PUNISHED?" she stormed. "Stand still, you weak-kneed dumbbells, you little empty-headed jugs!"

At that moment Flutter Mildweather stepped forward.

She was calm. She held her head high. Her cloak billowed as if it had come alive, and sunbeams seemed to shimmer on the butterfly wings decorating her hat.

Nana caught sight of her, turned her back, but didn't drop the children. An inexplicable, triumphantly malicious smile spread over her face. Her mouth twisted and her eyes glittered sharp as tacks.

She didn't look scared, hardly even surprised, merely scornful. She drew herself up, so powerful, so massive that next to her Flutter Mildweather seemed reduced to nothing. Whoever looked at them then would have had no doubt which was the stronger, which one would win.

The Lord and his Lady scarcely dared breathe as they stood watching.

But Flutter did not face them, so they were unable to see her eyes. Nor would they have been able to look, for no human being could have endured the expression in her eyes at that moment. No words can describe it.

Nana trembled, but still stayed firm. Her face was also terrible to behold, but it was, after all, only wicked, only evil, only cruel—whereas Flutter's eyes were like a tornado, a fire-spouting mountain, an earthquake. Yet all the while they remained the same peaceful, untroubled blue of a summer night sky. Her glance, her spirit, could never be quenched.

Now her voice could be heard, eternal, terrible, calm.

"Nana, children become what you make of them. Look at your empty-headed pupils."

Nana tried to overcome Flutter's stare, but then her eyelids began to jerk and twitch. She caught them a couple of times and managed to keep on staring back before she had to give up. Then she looked down at the children.

She backed away violently. The evil expression in her eyes turned to fright.

Even the Lord and his Lady stood still as stones. They saw it all.

For Nana was holding onto the handles of two clay jugs. Klas and Klara were nowhere to be seen. They had vanished.

In that instant, Mimi shrieked. Her shriek was higher, more full of dread and horror than ever be-

fore. It was a waking scream this time, and caused a pain that was almost not of this world.

When it died away, a strange shattering tinkle of glass could be heard. Over all the House glass broke into smithereens. So shattering, so totally shattering, was that scream, that it crashed all the mirrors and all the window panes.

With their hands full of fragments, the Lord and his Lady stood there. The bowls they were holding had broken before their very eyes.

The Lady began to sob quietly.

In that instant everything stopped. A stillness fell as if nothing in space existed, only eternity. It was as if life couldn't start up again. As if, when Mimi screamed, everything had stopped.

But then Wise Wit rose up and glided silently through the room. He reached Mimi's cage and opened it with his beak.

Mimi flew out. Straight into the light, and out through the recently shattered window panes, through the tangled creeper vines, out into the free wind she rose, higher and higher into space . . . in pure joy. She didn't look around, she just disappeared with a boundless, unending cry of joy.

Wise Wit watched her fly off from the window ledge, and when she had gone he explained, "In ancient times we were young together. We two can understand each other. . . ."

At his words, everyone in the room came to life

again. The Lord and his Lady turned to each other in confusion, and the Lord took her hands.

Nana seemed to have completely lost her mind, for she wandered around witlessly, tearing up her belongings, muttering mysteriously to herself. She left the room in a panic, but then returned immediately. Her eyes searched around the room and rested on Flutter. She went up to her and their eyes met, but without hatred now. The power had gone from Nana—she had given up.

As if it were very obvious, she said to Flutter, "We'll meet again, sister."

And Flutter nodded wearily.

"Yes," she replied, "we'll meet again. . . ."

And then Nana left.

But the Lady leaned against the Lord and sobbed and sobbed. He stroked her hair but looked equally downcast himself. For he wasn't wicked and he couldn't rid himself of the picture in his mind of the jugs that Flutter Mildweather had just taken, one under each arm.

"It is all my fault," he repeated, "my fault, my fault. Who can ever forgive me. . . ."

"Poor little children," sobbed the Lady. "Will they ever return to life again? Do they have to be jugs forever now, Mademoiselle?"

Flutter Mildweather stopped before them on her way out of the room. Her strange eyes were full of compassion.

154

"No, not forever and ever," she said. "Only as long as they remain here, for here in this house they cannot be anything else."

"But if they were to go home?" asked the Lord anxiously.

"Yes, then they would be children again."

And then the Lord said something he thought he would never ever say again. He said, "Thank you."

And the Lady whispered falteringly, "I wish . . . I wish you happiness."

"I wish the same for you, my Lady," said Flutter, and then walked over to the door. There she turned and called out, "And for you too, my Lord."

Then the Lord said thank you a second time. It was the first time Flutter Mildweather had called them my Lord and my Lady, whatever that may mean. . . .

Wise Wit spread out his wings, and flapped protectively over her head, and Flutter walked through the House carrying the clay jugs. She was exhausted.

The House had so many rooms and stairs. Too many.

In one room she came upon the old coachman, who stood there bending stiffly over a round table on which twelve glasses lay shattered in a ring around the rim. His shadow fell over the white tablecloth like the hands of a clock that had stopped forever.

Flutter Mildweather walked over to him and touched him.

"There's no need to brood over that any more," she said gently. "A bird's cry has been breaking the glass this time. Not the little boy. But the bird has flown off now, and the children are gone. It will never happen again. . . ."

But the coachman neither heard nor saw her. He was old; he stood still and the hands of the clock now pointed to seven.

Flutter Mildweather saw it was evening already. They had to hurry.

She left the House by a back door. She didn't want

to leave through the town gates, but instead used a smaller door in the wall, which opened directly onto the River of Forgotten Memories. There a little boat was moored.

She hopped down into it and rested the jugs in the bow, while Wise Wit perched in the stern.

She untied the boat and let it glide out into the river.

The breezes of day had died down; the water was calm. She sat a while quite still, resting on her oars as the sun set.

The House was reflected in the water. And that was just how the House should look! It shimmered and shivered until the boat slowly slipped out across the reflection as if through a dream.

She began to row as the dusk fell. Rowing felt good to her now.

The river was deep and hid many forgotten memories. Those that had sunk there were lost forever. Flutter knew this.

And when she reached the other bank, she also knew that everything had been accomplished. She laid down her oars and turned slowly around.

It was exactly as she had thought.

Klas and Klara lay asleep in the bow. There was not a trace of the clay jugs. She took a little rug that lay in the boat and spread it over the children. Wise Wit watched her carefully.

"You bewitched them," he said.

"I changed their appearance," she answered.

"They changed . . . but I trust you didn't change as well."

"Yes, I had to see the same thing I wanted the others to see. The jugs were an illusion, for they have been children all the time."

The raven nodded wisely.

"Wise Wit knew that and wasn't a bit confused," he announced.

Flutter smiled and looked at him for a long time, but said nothing more. Then she tied the boat to a tree and lay down in the hull, wrapped in her cape. Wise Wit was already asleep, with his head tucked under his wing.

They would continue their journey in the morning, but now they must rest.

It will be nice to start weaving again, thought Flutter Mildweather. That's really all I would like to do now. I hope I won't have to tell fortunes any more or do any more witchcraft. I know better than that. This time it was necessary, but in fact you shouldn't really ever let your shuttle run into other people's tapestries. . . ."

The boat rocked and bobbed so gently in the water.

Soon Flutter Mildweather was sleeping, too. Her hat lay beside her, and the night breezes played with the butterfly wings. She smiled gently in her sleep but didn't dream.

Part
Three

"... if it so happens
that you get what you desire,
then it is as fate has decreed."
GROA'S MAGIC FORMULAS

20

THE DOLL SHOP was the first place Sofia caught sight
of when she came to the fair. She felt a pang of grief,
and didn't dare look at the dolls. All she wanted to
do was get away from there.

But she couldn't help her eyes being drawn to the
shop, and her heart pounded with fright. Once more
she experienced that terrible day when the children
had disappeared. Couldn't she be spared that?

For in the same place, in the very same corner of
the doll shop, hung a doll absolutely identical to the
one Klara had longed for that time years ago. The
doll with the black satin cloak, the long golden
braids, and the lilac kerchief. The doll that the old
lady had insisted that Klara had bought just before
she disappeared. It was hanging there right now.
Sofia stared at it, bewitched and terrified out of her
wits, as if it had been a ghost. The doll swung back
and forth on its little strings, and Sofia got the impression that it was looking at her with its bright
blue-button eyes.

She rushed away in complete terror. She wouldn't say anything to Albert. Why should she dredge up sorrow for him, too, when it did no good? He was so gloomy and melancholy all the time now, anyway. Nor had she told him anything about her night visit with the ring to Flutter Mildweather. Why should she rouse the same illusion of hope in him that she had once felt herself?

She had believed so blindly in Flutter Mildweather, and she still did, even now, sometimes. But an ugly doubt had begun to appear. Perhaps all Flutter had wanted was her ring; perhaps that's why she offered to help. Though Sofia put aside the thought, still it returned.

She ran back and helped Albert in his shop. His glassware was in great demand now, as usual.

It was summer, and the sun shone warmly. A crowd of happy people milled around, looking forward to the evening's pleasures.

But when Albert had finished selling his glassware that afternoon, Sofia wanted to start back home. What else was there for them to do at the fair? They couldn't feel very joyful. They didn't want to join in the amusements.

Albert agreed with her. It was better to travel home. They would have fine weather for their journey. They could let the horse trot along all night if necessary, as long as they didn't have to stay in the fairground and feel bored and out of place.

He gathered up his things in the shop and they

walked over to pack their wagon, which stood with the others near the woods surrounding the fairground.

They walked past a bush that overhung a stone wall. Some gypsies had thrown things over the bush. Their wagons were nearby, and here they dried their patched laundry out in the sun.

They heard music from one of the wagons. Someone was playing artlessly, a melancholy tune. Someone was playing all alone as they walked past.

A little further off sat a raven that had flown up onto the stone wall. He sat perfectly still and studied his shadow solemnly as they passed by. He wasn't frightened by them and didn't fly away when he saw them.

"Isn't that Flutter Mildweather's one-eyed raven?" asked Albert, pausing. But then the raven lifted its head, and he noticed that it had two eyes.

"No," he said. "It can't be. This one had two eyes."

He wanted to walk on, but Sofia stayed there. She took a step nearer the wall and looked up at the raven thoughtfully. There was something so familiar about the bird. It turned one eye to her and studied her with an expression she couldn't understand, for she had met that look before, but didn't remember where. Her heart began to pound faster in her breast. The raven's eye was green. It blinked. She felt dizzy, with a strange sense of unreality. It couldn't be so.

And yet she knew right off that that mysterious

green glance had stared at her in the moonlight
once before and blinked then just as it did now. She
recognized it: the ring's shifting green stone that
had always upset her, that had always reminded her
of a wild creature's eye—a bird's eye.

Was it Wise Wit's eye?

Through her mind rushed everything she had ever
heard about Wise Wit. He had lost his one eye when
he had gazed too deeply into the well of wisdom, so
people said. But she had never believed that.

They also said he had lost his night eye, the bad
eye. And so he had only been able to see the light,
the beautiful and the good. He hadn't even been
able to see his own shadow.

But this raven was busy studying his own shadow.
He could really see it. And he saw more than that.
He had an eye that had seen down into the depths of
wisdom. Sofia knew that now. It was Wise Wit's eye.

And that was why the ring had given her no
peace. For who could wear Wise Wit's eye on her
finger? The thought made her feel dizzy.

The sun was about to set. It spread out its evening
light with a sudden, mighty, bursting display that
dazzled them. The whole sky suddenly blazed with
light. The stone wall where Wise Wit sat turned red.
The road glowed golden.

Stillness fell over the district. Even the commotion
in the fairground was hushed. Only the same lonely
person in the gypsy wagon went on playing. But his

melody began to change, the tones fought a jumbled battle with each other, in which sadness and melancholy changed into a strong tune of joy.

The tune was neither beautiful nor particularly well played. It was plucked by dirty fingers on a simple fiddle, but it grew into a melody that nothing in the world could overcome because it was so truly happy.

Wise Wit felt compelled to follow suit. He lifted his wings and flew right up into the sky.

Albert took Sofia's hand and pressed it tightly.

Because now they could see who was playing. He stepped out of the wagon and sat down on a stone among the blossoming hop vines in the hedge. It was a little old man, frightfully little, almost a dwarf. His hair and beard fringed his whole face and shone in the glow of the sunset. He was ancient.

It was the little old man who had sold Albert the ring for Sofia.

But he didn't see them; he just went right on playing.

Then, in the middle of the golden road, Albert and Sofia saw two little children wandering along. Behind them walked Flutter Mildweather. They saw her billowing cloak and her fluttering hat silhouetted against the sun, but when she caught sight of them, she turned and disappeared.

The children went on walking by themselves. Albert and Sofia ran toward them. They were Klas and

Klara. They were walking quite peacefully, not at all changed from when they had last been seen so very long ago.

Right there on the road they held the children close in their arms for a long time. Not a word was said, but after a while Klara took Sofia eagerly by the hand and led her away, just as she had done once before.

"We have to go look for the doll, mother," she said. "Do you think she's still there?"

And then Albert and Sofia realized that the children had forgotten everything that had happened to them while they were away. And they marveled how this could be.

For how could Albert and Sofia know that those who row across the River of Forgotten Memories

never remember what happened to them on the
bank they have left behind? They can only remember what happens on the other bank, the one they
land on.

Klas and Klara would never remember the House;
they would not remember the Lord, nor his Lady,
nor even Nana.

It had all sunk forever in the River of Forgotten
Memories.

But sometimes they would wonder why they were
scared when they walked on high flights of stairs. Or
why they sometimes ran up to a mirror with their
hearts in their mouths, for fear they would find the
mirrors empty. Why were they always so very happy
when they could see their reflections?

Once or twice, out of the blue, they woke in the
middle of the night and thought they were chained
tightly to a giant. But then Sofia lit a candle and
said that it was just something they had been
dreaming.

"Dreams are like streams," she would whisper
gently in their ears. "Dreams flow away like
streams. . . ."

And then they would forget again. . . .

It was a dream—nothing more.

But that evening, in the radiant sunset, they didn't
think of such things.

They walked with their mother and father around
the fairground. They watched the dancing bears and

the girls dancing on stilts. They rode on the carousel, and they were given presents.

All the dolls in the doll shop had been sold—except the doll with the golden braids, the satin cloak, and the lilac kerchief.

The old lady in the shop was bewildered. She was astonished. She hadn't noticed that doll at all, she said. And she knew for sure that she hadn't made a doll like that for this year's fair. It was a mystery to her how it came to be there. But what did that matter to Klara and Sofia!

And so everything turned out as it was supposed to. When Klara felt the doll in her arms, everything was just as it should be. The circle was closed, and everything was back to normal again. No one needed to know more. And no one understood any more, either.

Of course Flutter Mildweather knew. It was her fate to know and understand more than other people did.

That evening she stood once again out under her apple tree. The blossoms were over now, but she saw that it would bear a great harvest of fruit that autumn, more than she would ever be able to count.

It would be a good year, she could tell.

"Wise Wit," she called thoughtfully to the raven perched up in the tree. "Do you know now . . . or not?"

"Yes, I know," replied the raven.

They looked at each other.

"Your eye turned green from lying so long in wisdom's well. . . ."

"I know that," said Wise Wit.

"What more do you know?"

The raven fell silent and then gave her a moongaze and answered, "Everything. Before the sun knew where it lived, before the moon knew what power it possessed, before the stars knew where they should shine, Wise Wit knew the whole of life."

Flutter Mildweather listened thoughtfully and nodded at his words.

The raven was his old self again. He had his eye back, his dark eye of the past. Nothing would ever be hidden from him again. He could see ahead and backward in time the way he used to.

Now he looked at her with his other eye, the good eye, which she had not dared believe when it alone looked out on life. But now she could believe it, and it had a hopeful expression. She smiled . . . mint blue.

"So then I can get back to my weaving again," she said, entering her cottage.

Wise Wit remained up in the tree. He was listening.

He listened to the clatter of her loom. To the murmur of time. To the dew that fell on the grass.

MARIA GRIPE (1923–2007) was born Maja Stina Walter in Sweden's Stockholm archipelago, the daughter of an army captain. She attended Stockholm University, where she studied philosophy and the history of religion, and in 1946 married the artist Harald Gripe. Though she wrote stories from the time she was a child, Gripe did not publish her first book until she was thirty-one. Her first notable success came in the 1960s with a trilogy of books about Hugo and Josephine, and in 1964 she published *Glasblåsarns barn*, translated into English as *The Glassblower's Children* in 1973. In 1974 she received Hans Christian Andersen Award, the most prestigious prize given to a writer of children's literature. She adapted many of her books for radio, television, and film; in 1998 a movie adaptation of *The Glassblower's Children*, starring Stellan Skarsgård, was released. Among Gripe's books translated into English are *The Night Daddy*, *Elvis and His Secret*, and *Agnes Cecilia*.

HARALD GRIPE (1921–1992) was born and raised in Stockholm. Early in his career he worked as a set designer but later focused on painting and the illustrations he drew for his wife's many books, working frequently in the style of white line etched into a dark background. His large collection of toy theaters is displayed at Gripe Model Theater Museum in Nyköping, Sweden, where he and Maria lived for most of their married life.

RHODA LEVINE and EDWARD GOREY
He Was There from the Day We Moved In
Three Ladies Beside the Sea

JOHN MASEFIELD
The Box of Delights
The Midnight Folk

WILLIAM McCLEERY and WARREN CHAPPELL
Wolf Story

E. NESBIT
The House of Arden

DANIEL PINKWATER
Lizard Music

ALASTAIR REID and BEN SHAHN
Ounce Dice Trice

BARBARA SLEIGH
Carbonel and Calidor
Carbonel: The King of the Cats
The Kingdom of Carbonel

FRANK TASHLIN
The Bear That Wasn't

VAL TEAL and ROBERT LAWSON
The Little Woman Wanted Noise

JAMES THURBER
The 13 Clocks
The Wonderful O

ALISON UTTLEY
A Traveller in Time

T. H. WHITE
Mistress Masham's Repose

MARJORIE WINSLOW and ERIK BLEGVAD
Mud Pies and Other Recipes